TURNS
ON A DIME

JULIE LAWSON

TURNS
ON A DIME

*Best wishes
Ashley,*

Stoddart Kids

TORONTO • NEW YORK

*We acknowledge the Canada Council for the Arts and the Ontario Arts Council
for their support of our publishing program.*

*The author gratefully acknowledges support
from the British Columbia Arts Council.*

Published in Canada in 1998 by
Stoddart Kids,
a division of Stoddart Publishing Co. Limited
34 Lesmill Road
Toronto, Canada M3B 2T6
Tel (416) 445-3333 Fax (416) 445-5967
E-mail: Customer.Service@ccmailgw.genpub.com

Published in the United States in 1998 by
Stoddart Kids
a division of Stoddart Publishing Co. Limited
180 Varick Street, 9th Floor
New York, New York 14207
Toll free 1-800-805-1083
E-mail gdsinc@genpub.com

Distributed in Canada by
General Distribution Services
30 Lesmill Road
Toronto, Canada M3B 2T6
Tel (416) 445-3333 Fax (416) 445-5967
E-mail:
Customer.Service@ccmailgw.genpub.com

Distributed in the United States by
General Distribution Services
85 River Rock Drive, Suite 202
Buffalo, New York 14207
Toll free 1-800-805-1083
E-mail gdsinc@genpub.com

Canadian Cataloguing in Publication Data

Lawson Julie, 1947–
Turns on a dime

ISBN 0-7737-7464-0

I. Title.

PS8573.A94T87 1997   jC813'.54   C97-93065-6
PZ7.L38Tu 1997

Cover and text design: Tannice Goddard

Printed and bound in Canada

For Kay and Carl —
memories of the Southern Cross

Acknowledgements

My thanks to Don Campbell, Firearms Officer (retired) of the B.C. Ministry of the Attorney General, for providing information about the Webley revolver and answering my questions so patiently. I'm also grateful to him for reading, in draft form, the excerpts pertaining to the revolver. His comments were helpful, and greatly appreciated.

To Kevin Major, who read an earlier version of the manuscript — many thanks for your insightful comments and encouraging words.

And a special thanks to Patrick Lawson, whose patience and encouragement helped me through the twists and turns of this book.

Author's Note

Turns on a Dime is the second book in a trilogy. It began with *Goldstone*, a work inspired by actual events that took place in British Columbia at the turn of the century.

Turns on a Dime is a work of fiction. The characters and events — with the exception of the historical Rogers Pass Slide — are the product of my imagination or are used fictitiously. Any resemblance to actual persons living or dead, or events, is entirely coincidental.

1

Jo was mowing the lawn when Susan MacKenzie Lamont came home. Mowing the lawn and talking out a story.

"In my family," she was saying to herself, *"there's a story that makes me shiver."*

The chatter of the lawn mower blades hid the sound of her voice. None of the neighbors across the picket fence could hear — not Mrs. Miller, hanging the wash on her squeaky clothesline, not Mr. Jordan, polishing his brand-new '57 Thunderbird, not the little kids playing cops-and-robbers. Not even Flicka, the golden retriever dozing on Jo's back porch.

"Makes me shiver?" Jo tasted the words. "No . . . *Gives* me the shivers. That sounds better."

How much time did she have? Six weeks till the end of June, two weeks till the deadline. Plenty of time to work out the story, write it down, enter it in the contest. And win.

She pushed hard on the lawn mower's smooth wooden handle, whirring up a confetti of blossoms and fallen petals — pink, orange, yellow — and the spring-green scent of freshly-cut grass.

"*The story happened* — when was it? Some time in the early 1900s. OK. *The story happened a long time ago. Grandad Anderson was working for the railway in the Selkirk Mountains, near the Rockies . . .*"

Jo pulled back, struggled against a stubborn patch of dandelions, then started another row. Straight line along the edge of the vegetable garden. Turn at the raspberry canes. Straight line back towards her white stucco house with the dark green trim.

"*One night,*" she continued, "*Grandad was out clearing the tracks after an avalanche. The wind howled and roared and shrieked. Blizzards of snow whirled down from the mountain.* No, wait. *Whirled down from the dark night sky.* Yes!" The story was shaping up nicely. "*About midnight, my grandad —*"

The back door slammed. "Hey, Jo! Guess what?"

Jo looked up as her younger brother, Ian, clattered down the stairs, followed by an exuberant Flicka. "Mack's home!" he exclaimed.

The family story fled from Jo's mind. "What? Already?"

Mack and her parents had gone to Toronto in April for an extended family visit, and Jo hadn't expected

2

them back before the end of May. She resisted the impulse to bolt from the yard, run next door and attack Susan MacKenzie Lamont with one gigantic hug. Later, she would. But first . . .

She strained to push the lawn mower. Three more rows should do it. Then she would practice the piano, as planned.

"Well? Are you coming?" Ian gave her an impatient nudge. "Hurry up!"

"I'm almost done. Then I have to practice."

"*Jo-o!* You can do that later."

"All right. But I still have to get ready."

"Get ready? Why?"

"Because! I'm going to see Mack!"

Three rows later, Jo was in her room searching for something to wear. Flowered skirts and crinolines, cotton blouses, shorts . . . She pulled on a pair of striped navy-and-white pedal pushers, found a blue top to match and rummaged through her jewel case. A bracelet? No, the necklace of red and yellow pop-it beads Mack had given her. She put it on, decided it was too long and snapped off a dozen beads. Then she brushed her brown hair, tied it in a ponytail, and gave herself a critical look in the mirror.

"Knock, knock!" Ian banged at the door. "Jo, I'm going without you."

"Wait for me outside." Her heart was racing. Calm down, she told herself. It's only Mack. Beautiful and perfect Susan MacKenzie Lamont, otherwise known as Mack. Six years older than Jo, but her best friend in the entire world.

She flipped her ponytail and went outside to join her brother.

"About time," he said.

Jo looked at the house next door. Mr. Lamont's car was in the driveway, but Mack was nowhere to be seen. "I thought you saw her."

"I did," said Ian.

"Where did she go?"

"Inside."

"What did she look like?"

"Like Mack! Who else?"

Just then the door opened and Mack appeared. "Hi! You two coming over?"

"Sure!" Ian ran across the yard.

Jo followed more slowly. She felt shy suddenly, as if she should have grown up in the few weeks Mack had been away. As if she should have caught up to her somehow, instead of staying eleven.

"Don't mind the mess," Mack was saying as she led them into her room. "I've got all this unpacking to do." She bent down and started rummaging through one of the boxes on the floor. "Don't know why I took so much stuff. Maybe I secretly wanted to stay. Mom and Dad didn't. They hated Toronto. That's why we're back two weeks ahead of schedule. Soon as my cousin's wedding was over, Dad said, 'Time to hit the road.' And that was that. Here, Jo." She handed Jo a pile of books. "Put these in the bookcase, will you? Top shelf, with the other school books. I did all my homework in between wedding showers and family reunions and being polite to the relatives. I even did some babysitting."

"You used to babysit us," Ian said. "Every Friday night."

Mack laughed. "You make it sound like I've been away for years."

"You used to bring all that great stuff with you. That bag of tricks, remember?" Ian's face split in a grin. "The best times were the Choose Days —"

"— that you used to think were Tuesdays."

"And we had to pick one crumpled bit of paper out of a pile, and whatever we picked — that's what we got to do. Once we got to make fudge and another time we played Monopoly till midnight. Remember? And remember when . . ."

Jo tuned him out. She ran her fingers over the spines of Mack's books — mysteries, fairy tales, horse stories. When Jo had borrowed and read them all, Mack had started taking her downtown to the library. Every Saturday morning.

"Hey, Mack?" Ian said. "Remember on Jo's birthday you made that — what was it called? That fancy cake thing, with the sparkler?"

"Baked Alaska! That was my gourmet stage."

"And you taught us how to say Bun Appay Treat."

Bon appétit. Jo remembered. It was her eighth birthday, and Mack had surprised her with Baked Alaska, a Fantasyland concoction swirling with snowy peaks of meringue. On the outside, hot melt-in-your-mouth meringue. On the inside, the surprise of still-frozen ice cream. They had talked about Alaska, and Mack had said she wanted to go there — anywhere — to get away from boring Victoria.

Jo glanced at Mack, still playing "remember when" with Ian. She looked the same, with her green eyes and long blonde ponytail. Her smile was friendly, she laughed in all the right places. But there was an edge to her, a polish that seemed too bright. Was she happy to be back? Or was she anxious to leave again? She'll really think Victoria's boring now, Jo thought, especially after being in a big city like Toronto. And after being with her big-city cousins, she'll probably think I'm boring, too.

"Jo, wake up! You look like you're lost in another world. Here, can you put this on my dresser?" Mack reached across the bed and handed Jo a small pink jewel case.

"My favorite!" Jo opened the lid and a tiny ballerina appeared, dancing to a tinkling waltz above the sparkle of rings, brooches and necklaces. "You took this all the way to Toronto?"

"Sure did," Mack said. "Couldn't decide what dazzling jewels to wear, so I took everything."

Jo was surprised Mack had any jewelry left. "It's Choose Day," she used to say, opening the case. "Take whatever you like."

Once, Jo had picked out a brooch shaped like a sword from *The Arabian Nights*. "It even comes out of the scabbard," she'd said delightedly.

"It's called a scimitar," Mack had explained. "Isn't that a magical word?"

As she placed the jewel case on the dresser, Jo looked at Mack's smiling face and remembered thinking how wonderful it would be to grow up and be beautiful like her. And to know everything there was to know. "I've still got it," she said. "The scimitar brooch, I mean. I wear it all the time. And you know the gold chain that attaches the sword to the scabbard? It's never been broken."

"Good," said Mack.

"And it won't be, either," Jo added emphatically. She knew the chain was delicate, and handled it with care.

2

Jo did not let Mack's homecoming stand in the way of her story. Biking to and from school, watching TV with her friends Sharon and Wendy, drying the supper dishes, playing the piano, gazing at the stars from her bedroom window — no matter what she was doing, the story rolled in her head and onto her tongue. Even after she wrote it down, she talked it out. Then she'd go back to her exercise book, add a sentence, scratch out a few words, scribble some more. When it was perfect, she rolled a sheet of paper into Mom's typewriter, switched the ribbon from red to black so it would look professional, and laboriously — with two fingers — typed the good copy.

Mom, Dad, her grandparents — everyone who

read it was impressed. Even Mr. West, her teacher. "Well done," he'd said. "You've got an excellent chance with this one."

Three weeks later, Jo sat cross-legged on the floor of the school auditorium, petrified. Any minute now, the stern-looking man in the light brown suit would go to the microphone and say, "The winner of this year's Composition Award is" — pause for dramatic effect — "Joanne Gillespie!" She would stand to thunderous applause, walk confidently to the stage, shake the man's hand (what was the Superintendent of the School Board, anyway?), graciously accept the prized certificate with the gold seal, and return to her spot on the floor.

All morning, she and her fellow students had been crushed in the auditorium, clapping through the annual year-end awards ceremony, praying their name would be called for something, *anything*, trying not to feel the heat, trying not to squirm, because if you did, eagle-eyed Mr. West would zap you with his famous look.

Jo tentatively shifted her position, careful not to poke the person in front. If she had to stand now, the pins and needles would shoot up her legs and she'd topple over, disgracing herself in front of everybody. Or her skirt would ride up somehow and she'd die of embarrassment.

Wait. The time had come. Oh, *please*, she prayed as the man from the School Board began to speak.

". . . and we all want to stress the value of good composition, *blah, blah, blah* . . ."

School *Bored* was more like it. What was he going on about?

". . . and the wonderful theme of this year's contest — Family Stories."

Jo's heart pounded. Her cheeks turned red with anticipation. Beside her, Sharon whispered, "Good luck, Jo."

Jo whispered back, "Thanks. Same to you."

Mr. West caught her eye and gave her a warm smile.

". . . and what a wide range of responses," the man droned on. "But none so *something, something* as this year's winner."

Jo smoothed her skirt, steeled herself to stand —

And heard the name.

"It's not me!" The words slipped out, unnoticed. Incredibly, the thunderous applause was for a grade seven girl who walked confidently to the stage and accepted the award.

"It was very close," Mr. West said when they returned to the classroom. "I know how disappointed you are, Jo, but you'll have another chance next year. And don't forget, we have our own awards after lunch. Much classier, I might add. We've even got refreshments."

"It's not fair," Jo said. "Just because I'm in grade six. And next year there'll be a different topic. I might not know what to write."

Mr. West patted her shoulder. "You'll think of something. You always do."

At least for the class awards you didn't have to sit on the floor and listen to a bunch of boring speeches. Everyone got something, even if it was for Perfect Attendance or Best Excuse for Late Homework.

Near the end of the afternoon, Mr. West announced that there were three awards for Best Composition. But before presenting them, he wanted the class to hear the winning stories. Everyone clapped as Sharon, then Bob, read theirs.

"And finally," Mr. West said, "let's have a big hand for our first prize winner, Joanne."

Jo walked to the front of the room. She took a deep breath, faced her classmates, and in a clear voice that belied her nervousness, began to read.

My Family Story

In my family, there's a story that gives me the shivers. Whenever my dad hears it, he says, "That's life. It can turn on a dime." Whenever I hear it or think of it, I wonder, "What if?"

The story happened a long time ago. My Grandad Anderson was a roadmaster for the Canadian Pacific Railway. He was working in the Selkirk Mountains. One night, he and his crew were in Rogers Pass, clearing the tracks after an avalanche. The site was lit up brighter than a city with torches and lanterns and lights from the snowplow and locomotive. The men were down in the cut, digging away, while the wind howled and snow swirled around their heads. Just before midnight, Grandad decided to phone in a report. He hiked away down the tracks to a watchman's shack, made the phone call, warmed himself by the fire and

11

talked to the watchman. Then he trudged back wearily through the snow.

When he reached the slide site, everything was gone. The lanterns were gone, the light from the snowplow was gone, the locomotive was gone. And all the men were gone. Another avalanche had come down and buried everything. Grandad called out, "Is anybody alive?" One voice answered, "Over here!" Grandad stumbled through the snow and found a man half-buried. It was Bill LaChance, whose name is French for luck. He was the only man who survived the slide. Sixty-two men died. Including my grandad's brother.

My grandad is old now. When he tells me the story he has tears in his eyes. I know he doesn't like to remember. I try to imagine how he felt, that terrible night in the mountains when the lights went out in the snow. Seeing that darkness, hearing that one voice. I ask him, "What if you had waited, or come back too soon?" He says, "Things would have been different."

I ask him, "What made you go to the phone then?" He shrugs. But I know what he's thinking. He's thinking it's as if someone tapped him on the shoulder and whispered, "Now's the time."

I think it might have been an angel.

Everyone clapped when Jo finished reading. Gil flapped his arms as if they were wings and made what he thought was an angel sound. Jo ignored him, and graciously accepted her certificate from Mr. West.

"And a bonus," he said, "for the person who should have received the School Board Award — a

12

blank book for future compositions."

Jo thanked her teacher and, hugging the leather-bound book, returned to her seat. Gil was already striding up to accept his award as Best Joker, and the class was roaring with laughter at his latest joke. Why, Jo couldn't imagine. Probably because they understood it. His was a down-to-earth "Little Moron" story, not a "what if" kind of story like hers. It didn't matter. Her classmates never understood her, anyway.

Even the girls who called themselves her friends could "turn on a dime," as Dad would say. Sharon, for instance. She and Jo had known each other since kindergarten. They'd worked on school projects together, gone for bike rides, staged neighborhood plays. They'd even had the same piano teacher until Sharon got tired of practicing and quit.

Then, the previous summer, Wendy had moved into the neighborhood. For a while they were the "Three Musketeers," but before long, three became a crowd and Jo was the one left out.

The girls *said* they liked her, even invited her to their parties. When one was sick or busy, the other was quick to call Jo. But when they were together they often treated her as if she were from another planet.

Why? Jo wondered. Was she too serious? Too *square*? Did they think she was stuck-up because she didn't laugh at their jokes? Well, why should she? They weren't funny.

Or were the girls jealous? Moments ago, she'd noticed the look on Sharon's face when Mr. West had given Jo the special book. Sharon had entered that contest, too. Chances are she wasn't pleased to see Jo singled out as the person who should have won.

When the three o'clock bell rang, Jo raced down the stairs, hoping Mr. West wouldn't see her, then ran to the bike racks and rode away. At least the awards ceremony was over. She wouldn't have to sit through that for another year. In three days, school would be over. And Mack was back.

She swerved to avoid the black cat crossing the road. How had the time passed so quickly? And who cared? The important thing was sooner or later it passed.

"Fudge, fudge, tell the judge, Mommy's got a new baby." She sang the skipping rhyme as she steered her bike off the pavement and into the woods for the shortcut home. *"It ain't no girl, it ain't no boy, it's just a newborn —"* Whomp! She hit a rock, swerved off the well-trodden path and bumped down a small slope. But she kept her grip, guiding the three-speed as if it were a tempermental stallion only she could handle.

Time passed, all right. As quickly as "red hot pepper," when they turned the skipping rope so fast it blurred. Jo loved skipping — the nonsense chants and the satisfying slap the rope made when it hit the pavement. Turning the rope was like the turning over of time. Turning back, turning forward, turning away from all the things she could never return to. It seemed like a minute ago it was spring. Now spring was over. And her piano exam was over. "I did well, too!" she announced to the blue camas lilies clustered beneath the garry oak trees. "The Kabalevsky 'Waltz' was perfect.

14

And I only stumbled once — nothing serious — in the Bach."

"Hey, Jo! Wait!"

Jo recognized the voices. She skidded to a stop and waited for the girls to catch up.

Sharon reached her first. "Nice prize," she said, eyeing the book safely tucked inside Jo's carrier. "Congratulations."

"Thanks!" Jo grinned. "Same to you. I liked your story."

Sharon shrugged. "Nah, it was nothing. Only second place. But we were wondering —" She giggled and turned to Wendy. "Go on, you tell her."

"No, you!"

Jo's hand flew to her face. Was there something on her nose? Or a tomato soup mustache left over from lunch? Was that why Gil and the other boys had snickered while she read her story?

Sharon kicked Jo's front tire. "It's about your bike. Why do you keep riding this old thing to school?"

"Yeah," said Wendy. "It's not, you know —"

"Cool. For grade seven."

Jo rolled her eyes and sighed. "I'm not *in* grade seven."

"You will be next year. You should start practicing."

"That's ridiculous." Jo started to get on her bike but Wendy grabbed her arm.

"Another thing." She poked at the rope wound up in the carrier. "How come you're still skipping at recess? With the grade fives? You're too old for that."

"Yeah," Sharon agreed. "Playing the piano is a

sissy enough thing without playing baby games."

"What?" Jo gaped. "What does playing the piano —"

"And about your story. That contest wasn't supposed to be a made-up family story. At least mine was true."

"Mine's true!"

"How can it be? There's no such thing as angels."

"Well, I think there is. At least the guardian angel kind. 'Cause if my grandad had died in the avalanche, then my mom wouldn't have been born. And if that hadn't happened, where would I be?"

"Who cares?" Sharon curled her lip in a sneer. "You'd be a nothing, like you already are."

"Just because your story didn't win!" Jo burst out angrily. "Anyway, the point of my story was how things happen by chance. Not whether or not there's angels. You missed the whole point."

"Ah, forget it." Laughing, the girls linked arms and continued along the path that led into Wendy's yard.

Jo felt a whomp in her stomach. What brought that on? Yesterday they'd been the best of friends. She'd gone to Wendy's after school and watched TV with her and Sharon. She'd even pretended to like their idol, Elvis Presley. She hadn't said anything to make them mad, had she?

Maybe it was the story contest and book prize. Or maybe they didn't need a reason. Sometimes they just felt like picking on someone. Like the boys did, with their stupid, horrible sharking.

Jo grimaced. Sharking happened whenever there was a new grade six or seven boy. If he wanted to fit in, he had to shark somebody. Which meant he had to take something from a girl. The other boys decided who and when and where. It hadn't happened to Jo yet, but she'd heard enough about sharking to be afraid. Not because something was taken, but because the girl it happened to was always alone and defenseless, surrounded by boys circling her like sharks.

The thought made her pedal faster, even though she knew she didn't have to worry. Not until September. And then, maybe Sharon or Wendy would get sharked. It would serve them right.

She left the path, bounced onto the pavement, and headed up the hill where she lived. Flicka, who had been waiting in the middle of the road, yapped a greeting, her tail wagging like red hot pepper.

"Hi, Flicka!" Jo's voice rose an octave. "Oh, you are such a good girl. Yes, yes, you are." She wheeled her bike across the lawn, leaned it against the weeping willow tree, then bent down and scratched Flicka behind the ears. "You don't care if I play the piano, do you? Or ride my old bike?" She pressed her cheek against the smooth fur. "We don't care what those morons think, do we, girl? No."

"What morons?"

Jo turned to Ian, working on his bike in the driveway. "Sharon and Wendy. Who else?" She watched him take a shiny green milk bottle cap and fold it around a bicycle spoke. Other spokes had blue, red, gold or silver, carefully arranged in patterns. "What are you doing after this?"

"Going to Wayne's. Why?"

"Thought you might want to do something with me. Bike to the store, get a popsicle . . ." She took a red foil cap and folded it around a spoke. "Knock knock."

"Who's there?"

"Dwayne."

"Dwayne who?"

"Dwayne the bathtub, I'm dwowning." She folded on a silver cap. "Can I have the leftovers for my bike?"

"I already said Wayne could have them. Sorry."

"Wayne, Duh-wayne." She scrunched up a circle of blue foil and threw it at him. "Thanks for nothing."

"Stop it! I'm telling Mom if you don't quit bugging me."

"Go ahead. She doesn't care. She's not your real mom. Dad's not your dad. And I'm not your sister, thank heavens."

Ian peered through the spokes. "What do you mean?"

"I found you on the porch one morning, tucked inside a basket. You were ugly, all red and squishy and wrinkled."

"I don't believe you." He turned back to the spokes, rearranging the foil caps Jo had put on.

"It's true," she said. "You were just born, and so tiny your head was the size of a walnut."

"How did I get there? Since you're so smart."

"Your real mother was taking you to the orphanage. People do that sometimes, when they don't want their baby."

"Like they did with you?"

"No, I made that up. The true story is your mom was struggling up the hill to get you to the orphanage before you froze —"

"It was winter?"

"The dead of. But she couldn't make it that far, she was so weak and tired. I picked up the basket to carry you inside, but it was heavier than I thought." Jo gave him a sad smile. "I didn't mean to drop you. I'm sorry."

"You *dropped* me?"

"I was only three. You landed on your little walnut head, that's why it's cracked. That's why there's a bit of brain damage."

"I don't believe you."

"Go ahead, ask Mom. Ask Dad. Would they lie to you?"

"How come my birthday's in June, not in the winter?"

"Because my birthday's in the winter. Dad's is in the fall and Mom's is in the spring. They wanted one birthday every season, to spread out the celebrations. That's why. So you got summer."

"I still don't believe you. Everyone says you make up stories and it's true."

"Who's everyone?"

"Everyone on the whole street, that's who."

"You're going to believe them and not your own sister?"

"You said you weren't my sister. See? I knew you were making it up." He hopped on his bike and tossed her a "gotcha!" grin. There was a blur of spinning colors as he rode off, and a soft ratchety sound, the flap-flap of foil caps.

It was true she told stories, but so what? That's why Mr. West had given her the book. Not just for her family story but for all the others she'd written during the year.

Mack liked her stories. Better yet, Mack had told her she had a way with words and should one day become a writer. And whatever Mack said was good enough for her.

3

"Soup's on!" Dad called from the dining room. "First day of summer holidays, and we've got a blue plate special."

Jo hurriedly finished the Beethoven piece she'd memorized for her piano exam, pleased that her fingers still remembered where to go. Then she plunked herself down at the table and eyed her mother's casserole. Dough-wrapped rolls of deviled ham nestled on a bed of vegetables and noodles, smothered in cream of mushroom soup. "Looks good, Mom. Is it a *Chatelaine* Meal of the Month? Or is that a silly question?"

Ian wagged a finger. "Silly question."

Ever since they'd given Mom a subscription to *Chatelaine* magazine, she'd been following the day-by-day suggestions for lunch and supper.

"We know you like the present, Mom," Jo said after the first month, "but you don't have to overdo it."

Some meals were better than others. The tuna fish salad wasn't bad. Neither were the breaded veal cutlets. But broiled perch with fresh spinach? Or lima bean casserole? Highly forgettable. Tonight's meal, on the other hand, looked scrumptious.

"Summer Pinwheel Casserole," Mom said proudly. "Didn't it turn out well?"

"Looks good enough to eat." Dad wasted no time digging in. "So how was your day, kids?"

"Good!" Ian said. "I finished reading the comic books Mack brought me from Toronto. *The Last of the Mohicans* and *Oliver Twist*. Mom, can she babysit again?"

"You don't need a babysitter," Mom pointed out. "Jo's old enough now. But if you want some company, Mack can certainly come over once our badminton starts up again in the fall. If she wants. And if you two don't mind."

"We don't, do we, Jo?"

Jo shook her head. Mind? She swallowed a mouthful of noodles and grinned like a Cheshire cat.

The next day, Jo was invited to listen to Mack's new records.

"It's probably Elvis Parsley," Ian said as she was leaving.

"Presley, for your information. Anyway, we won't be listening to that stuff. Something way better and you won't, so ha ha."

But Ian was right. Not only was Mack listening to the latest Elvis hit, she was making an Elvis collage on her wall. "Here," she said, handing Jo a pile of pictures. "You can tape these. Don't worry if they overlap." She pointed to a sultry Elvis. "I've seen him, you know."

"So have I," Jo said. "On TV. On 'The Ed Sullivan Show.'"

"No, I mean I've really seen him. When I was in Toronto. It was at a concert in Maple Leaf Gardens. This girl collected three thousand names on a petition begging Elvis to come to Toronto. And he did."

Jo frowned. This new Mack, gushing over a rock 'n' roll star, was so unlike the old Mack she didn't know what to say.

"It was way better than TV," Mack continued. "Did you know Ed Sullivan would only let him be filmed from the waist up? Well, take it from me, you have to see *all* of Elvis."

"Your parents let you go?"

"They didn't know. I told them I was going to a pajama party with my cousin. Which was true. Only first we all went to the concert."

"What did he sing?"

"Who knows? The screams drowned out his singing. Oh, it was wild! Now I've got all his records and a scrapbook filled with newspaper clippings. My parents think I'm demented, but it's not that bad. Some girls in Toronto were planning to break their legs, once they heard Elvis visited hospitals." She sighed. "I'll never date anybody who doesn't have sideburns."

"Does your dad let you go on dates now?" Jo wondered.

The winter Jo turned ten, Mack had taken her swimming at the Crystal Gardens Pool on Sunday afternoons. She always met somebody there, but swore Jo to secrecy. "I'm not allowed to date," she'd said. "I can't even talk to a guy on the phone."

"Why? You're old enough, aren't you? You're sixteen."

"Ha! If I was thirty I wouldn't be old enough," Mack had said. "My dad's what you might call overprotective."

Jo remembered how honored she'd been, having Mack trust her with a secret. She wondered if the need was still there. "Well, Mack? Does your dad let you or not?"

Mack winked and said nothing.

4

Alan didn't have sideburns. But he did have a '51 Chevy, so maybe that was enough for Mack. Like every other teenager at Willows Beach that summer, she thought his car was the coolest thing on the Esplanade.

Jo didn't think so. It was a yucky color, like green pea soup. But nobody asked her opinion.

She'd been thrilled when Mack invited her to Willows. It was a beautiful beach, only fifteen minutes away by bus. But Mack or no Mack, she hadn't left the sprinkler to walk on scorching pavement. She hated the Esplanade that curved along the sandy beach. It was crowded with teenagers, mostly boys, who sat on the railing and leered at the girls.

"Aren't we going on the beach?" Jo tried to sound indifferent. Whining would spoil everything.

"We'll have a look around first," Mack said. "See where the best place is, OK?"

A boy with his hair combed into a greasy ducktail whistled as they passed. Someone with a pimply face made kissing noises and called, "Hubba, hubba." Mack sauntered along unperturbed. Jo wished she were invisible. She wished it even more when Mack stopped at the end of the Esplanade.

"Half a sec', Jo, OK?" Without waiting for an answer, she joined the crowd clustered around a good-looking boy leaning nonchalantly against the door of a two-tone car.

Jo drummed her fingers on the railing while the noisy bantering filtered around her. Straight 6s, Flathead V-8s — what kind of language was that? She was about to say something when the boy spotted them. "Mack!" His tanned face cracked into a smile.

Mack blushed. "Hi, Alan. Fancy seeing you here."

"Quite a coincidence, all right. Long time no see."

"This your car?" Mack stepped forward and patted the pea green hood, then lightly ran her fingers over the beige roof.

"'51 Chevy, turtleback," he said proudly. "Only six years old. Want a ride?"

Mack looked at Jo and raised her eyebrows in a question. When Jo shook her head, she said, "Maybe later."

"You still babysitting?"

Mack laughed. "Jo doesn't need a babysitter. You

remember Alan, don't you, Jo? He used to be a life-guard at the Crystal."

Jo shrugged. "Not really."

Alan reached inside his car and took out a transistor radio. "Want to sit on the beach? I've got a place staked out."

Mack smiled, clearly delighted, and walked along beside him.

Jo trailed behind, stepping over logs, dried strands of seaweed and pieces of sun-bleached driftwood. Up ahead, Alan raved about his car. It was a wonder he was letting it out of his sight. And how come Mack was so interested? A year ago she had nothing but scorn for caraholics, as she called them. Now she hung onto every word, as if a Straight 6 was some exquisite brand of poetry.

Oh, well. At least she was here with Mack, not running through the sprinkler with Ian and Flicka. Sharon and Wendy would really think that was baby stuff.

Alan's spot was marked by a faded beach blanket and a windbreak. "What do you think? I built it myself out of driftwood."

Mack gave him an admiring smile. "You've been busy." She sat down and leaned against the log Alan had dragged over for a back rest. "It's wonderful."

Jo spread her towel beside the blanket, then stripped down to her bathing suit. She took off her canvas shoes and wiggled her toes in the sand. "Hey, Mack. Aren't you going swimming?"

"In a while." She fiddled with the dials on Alan's radio. "You go warm up the water for me."

27

Jo ran across the hot sand, dodging ducktails and bikinis, skirting little kids, jumping over beached logs and the turrets of sand castles. When she reached the water, she braced herself and plunged right in, flailing her arms and kicking out her legs. "Aughh!" she cried. "It's fuh-reeezing!" But the salt water felt good on her sweaty skin. Invigorating — once the initial shock had passed.

She floated on her back for a while, then switched to the frog kick and breast stroke Mack had taught her. "It helps firm up the pectoral muscles, as well as your arms and thighs," Mack had told her. "Keep practicing." Jo hadn't cared about pectoral muscles, whatever they were. She only wanted to swim like Mack.

Now she could. She put more energy into her strokes, scanning the shore until she spotted Mack, hoping Mack was watching. But the older girl was leaning on her elbow, laughing at something Alan had said. It didn't look as if she were all that keen on swimming.

"Want a ride home?" Alan asked when it was time to go.

"Better not," Mack said. "Some things never change."

"Why didn't we get a ride?" Jo wondered as they waited for the bus. She wouldn't have minded, even if the car was a putrid color. It would have given Wendy and Sharon something to talk about.

"Like I said, better not. Another time, maybe."

"Another time?"

"Sure! You're my beach buddy, now. For the whole summer."

Jo smiled. Thank heavens she hadn't whined.

Three days later, Jo was once again at Willows Beach. At least this time Mack was willing to walk on the sand. Good thing, too. Jo had spotted the pea green Chevy parked on the Esplanade, but so far, Mack hadn't noticed.

"Are you going to go swimming?" Jo asked.

"Sure," Mack said. "I'll keep you company. Soon as we get settled."

"OK." Jo hopped onto a long smooth log. Without losing her balance she walked the length of the log, then jumped onto another. She was congratulating herself, thinking it was time to try without looking at her feet, when she heard Mack laugh and say, "Well! What a coincidence!"

Jo stumbled and fell. Then she got up and saw Alan, leaning his perfect tan against his perfect log in his perfect windbreak.

"Hi, Mack!" he said. "You can sit here if you like. You too, Jo. There's plenty of room."

"Thanks! Unless . . ." Mack turned to Jo. "This OK with you?"

Jo shrugged. "I guess. Do you want to go swimming now?"

"No, I'll work on my tan for a while."

Jo left them listening to Alan's transistor and ran to the water. She swam, she helped two little kids with their sand castle, she collected shells. An hour later, she returned to the windbreak and tried again. "C'mon, Mack! The water's great!"

"Well . . ."

Alan got up and held out his hand. "Yeah, Mack. C'mon. I'll race you to the float."

That did it. Mack grabbed his hand and ran with him across the sand.

Jo followed. She watched as they raced to the float, knowing she couldn't swim out that far. So she splashed around for a while, then went back to the windbreak and changed the station on Alan's transistor. For a brief but satisfying moment, she thought about removing the batteries and burying them in the sand. Then she thought, don't be discouraged. There's always the next time.

But Alan was there the next time, too. And the time after that. Three times a week, except for a few rainy days and the week Jo went on holidays with her family, she and Mack took the bus to Willows Beach. Alan was always there. After the fifth time, Mack stopped saying, "What a coincidence." By then they were forever holding hands and making ga-ga eyes at each other.

Once, when Jo came back from swimming, she caught them talking about Mack's over-protective father. "Dad hit the roof that night you phoned," Mack was saying. "So you can imagine how he'd react if he saw us together."

"What if he saw us like this?" Alan leaned over to Mack and kissed her.

At the same time, Jo exclaimed, "Ohh! That's why Alan lets us out two blocks away, instead of driving us straight home. I thought so."

The lovebirds broke apart and stared at Jo as if

she'd just dropped in from Mars.

"Oops." Jo gave them a sheepish grin. "Sorry."

It wasn't always so bad. Alan bought her ice cream cones. And often, when they got back, Mack had a Choose Day, and let Jo pick something from her jewel case.

But after several weeks, Jo was becoming impatient. She was sick of hearing Alan talk about his high school soccer team, his plans for his Chevy, his night job as a car-hop. She was also sick of Mack coming into the water with her, only to swim off to the float with Alan.

So why do you go? Every time Mack invited her to the beach, Jo asked herself that question.

The answer was always the same. Because it was fun, most of the time. She liked the beach, she liked swimming, she liked being with Mack. And she didn't have to stay there. She was free to go home whenever she liked. Besides, there was always the chance Alan's car would break down or he'd be in a near-fatal accident and wouldn't show up at the beach.

"Don't you love walking barefoot?" Mack kicked up a spray of sand. Her toenails, painted flamingo pink, reminded Jo of tiny seashells. Her own toes looked more like ragged bits of cracked crab.

It was the middle of August, and Jo, Mack and Alan were heading for their usual spot.

"Walking barefoot is the best exercise for your feet," Mack was saying. "And it gets rid of dead skin from the soles."

Alan gazed at her as though she'd just spoken the

most amazing words in the history of the universe. Then he put his arm around her and nuzzled her ear.

"Oh, brother," Jo muttered. Things were getting worse.

After laying out the blanket and adjusting a few planks in the windbreak, Alan said, "Want some suntan lotion? You don't want to get burned." He spread it over Mack's bare shoulders and back, carefully avoiding the straps of her bathing suit. Mack closed her eyes, her lips curved in a scimitar smile. If she were a cat, Jo thought, she'd be purring.

"How about you, Jo?" Alan held out the lotion.

"No, thanks. I'm going swimming."

"Watch out for sharks."

Mack smiled sleepily. "Don't forget the pectorals."

"I won't." Jo ran to the water and plunged in, glad of the stinging cold. Pectorals. At least Mack hadn't said breast stroke in front of Alan. She would have died a thousand deaths.

And why did Alan have to mention sharks? Jo fought down the fear. There were two whole weeks before school. Two weeks and — she did a quick count — five days. Even then, sharking might not happen. And if it did, it wouldn't necessarily happen to her.

Reassured, she floated on her back with her eyes closed, kicking lazily, feeling the sun through her eyelids. Then she rolled over and stretched out her arms for the dead man's float. The brightness of the sun remained behind her eyes, even with her face under water.

When she returned, Mack and Alan were lying on

the blanket, so close you'd think they'd been poured out of the same bottle of suntan lotion. They were facing each other with such dreamy expressions Jo felt like throwing up. Instead, she picked up her towel and hurried to the change room.

Ten minutes later, they still hadn't moved. "Hey, Mack?"

"Hmm? Oh, hi. You're back. Have a good swim?"

"Yeah." Then she blurted out, "I'm going home now."

Mack sat up abruptly. "You're what?"

Her voice sounded unusually cross, but Jo plowed ahead. "I'll take the bus. I've got enough money."

"Alan will take us home."

"Yeah, but . . ." Jo shifted from one foot to the other, digging holes in the sand. "I feel like going home now."

"Wait, why don't you? Sit in the shade if you're too hot."

Jo felt her cheeks burning. "It's OK. I'll take the bus."

"If that's the way you want it." Mack smiled and waved, but the smile, Jo noticed, was for Alan.

5

The bus was pulling away from the curb when Jo reached the corner. Frantically, she broke into a run. "Stop! Wait!" she yelled.

The driver stopped and Jo got on. "Thank heavens," she gasped. She collapsed into a seat, relieved she didn't have to hang around for the next bus. It was way too hot.

Think cold, she told herself. Think snow.

As the bus groaned along the residential streets, Jo stared out the window and imagined snow. Snow covering the sun-baked lawns, snow burying the flower beds, snow changing the shape of the shady chestnut trees, snow piled on the roofs of the well-kept houses. And icicles — lovely, cold, delicious icicles — hanging from the eaves.

Victoria hardly ever had snow. Rain, fog, frost, and rain. Not much snow. Too bad, because the hill Jo lived on was perfect for tobogganing. The last time it snowed, *really* snowed, Dad was so excited he'd gone out and bought a toboggan for the family. That was five years ago, and they hadn't used it since.

It was because of the lack of snow that her grandparents had left the Selkirk Mountains, moved to Vancouver Island, and settled in Victoria. No snow, but no avalanches, either.

What would it be like to live in the mountains? Or up north, where the midnight sun in summer made up for the long dark winter? Grandma had told Jo that when she was a girl in Sweden, she used to dance in the midnight sun. That might make a good story, Jo thought. A romantic adventure, maybe? Or a mystery?

No, she decided. First I'll write a story about Mack. Let's see . . . *Mack is swimming at Willows Beach and gets a cramp. Oh no! She's sinking fast! Where's Alan, the lifeguard? He's off dusting his car! He doesn't even notice! So it's Jo to the rescue! Will she make it? Oh no! Mack's gone under again! Faster Jo, faster, work those pectorals —*

The bus braked suddenly, jolting her out of the story. She spotted the gray shingle house with the monkey tree and realized she only had three more stops to go. On the other hand, why not get off at the grocery store one stop after her own? It was a bit out of the way and would mean a longer walk home, but the afternoon would taste much better once she had a popsicle.

"Seven cents, please."

Jo handed the clerk the coins, then whacked the popsicle smartly against the side of the counter. As she was going out the door, she heard another sharp whack. She turned. A tall, slender boy around her own age, with blue eyes and reddish-brown hair gave her a freckled grin and proudly held up the two halves of his grape popsicle. "A brilliant execution," he said, falling in beside her. "How's your — what's this called?"

"A popsicle, what else?"

"In England we call it an ice lolly. Different shape, though."

"You're from England?" No wonder he talked funny.

"Brilliant deduction," he said. "So how's your popsicle?"

"Cold. How's yours?"

"Smashing, actually. I've never had grape before."

"Your lips and teeth are purple."

"You should talk." He laughed and pointed to her green mouth.

"Do you want to trade your other half, grape for spearmint?"

"No, thanks, I'll stay purple. Do you live around here? Stupid question. Why else would you be walking along this street? It's not exactly on the scenic route. I mean, it's not the Uplands, is it?"

"So? Who'd want to live in Snoblands anyway, with all the hoity-toity English?" She spoke in what she thought was a perfect imitation of Snob English, then realized what she'd said. "Oops, sorry. I forgot you were English."

"You are too, actually. I mean, you're not speaking Cantonese or Hungarian, are you? I'm *real* English, though. Not a generational transplant like you."

"A *what?*"

"A generational transplant. Your parents or grand-parents or great-grandparents came from England, whereas I, myself, came from England. Only a few weeks ago, actually. We came from London on a BOAC Comet 4. Are you impressed? That jet flies over eight miles a minute, so fast you can hardly even hear the sound of the engines. Light travels faster, though. One hundred and eighty-six miles a second. Have you ever been on a jet?"

"Hardly. Not from Victoria, the dead-end capital of the world. That's what Mack says. Full of newlyweds and nearly deads. But I like it."

"Who's Mack? Your brother?"

"No! Mack's a girl. She's seventeen and lives next door. I have a brother, but he just turned nine."

"You must be the same age as me. Twelve, right?"

"Not till December thirteenth. And this year my birthday falls on a Friday. But I'm not superstitious about it," she added, crossing her fingers. "Friday the thirteenth is usually a lucky day for me."

"My birthday's January the twenty-seventh and I'm going into grade seven at that school up the street."

"Same here! We might be in the same class!" On second thought . . . Jo glanced at him out of the corner of her eye. How would he fit in with Gil and Bob and the other grade seven morons? Heaven help him if he came to school in those ridiculous short pants. As for the la-de-da accent and the freckles . . .

"Quite a crop, isn't it? I'm glad you noticed."

Jo blushed furiously. "I wasn't —"

"I tried to count them but lost track after a hundred and seventy-nine. Or was it a hundred and ninety-seven? You wouldn't believe the skill required to produce such an outstanding crop. You don't have the skill, do you?" He peered at her face. "Hang on — there, below your eye. Is that a freckle? Or is it a mole?"

Jo hated her mole. Even pretending it was a beauty spot didn't help. "I wish I had an accent," she said, changing the subject.

"You do! I can hear it clearly."

"What does it sound like?"

"Canadian. Kind of flat, transplanted. Maybe even weed-like."

Jo laughed. This kid was a real character, as Dad would say. "You were wrong, you know. Just because I'm walking down this street doesn't mean I live around here. I could be in my grandparents' neighborhood, visiting them. And they're not transplanted English, they're Swedish."

"So you're part Swedish."

"Brilliant deduction," she mimicked. "I know some Swedish words too, like *flicka*. It means girl. That's what we call our dog. And my Grandad Anderson calls me *min lilla hönsa hoppa*. It means — promise you won't laugh — my little jumping hen. Or something like that."

The boy laughed. "Sorry. *Min lilla* —"

Jo whacked him one with her popsicle stick.

When they reached the corner, he slurped the last melting bite of popsicle and said, "Guess I'll see you in school. I'm turning up this street."

"This is *my* street!"

"You own it, then? We have to pay you rent to live here?"

"Hardly," she laughed. "See that house with the weeping willow? That's my house. And the golden retriever running down to meet me? That's Flicka. Aren't you, girl?" She stooped to retrieve the soggy tennis ball Flicka dropped at her feet.

"We've bought the house up the hill."

Jo stopped her arm in mid-throw. "The old Burgess house?"

"Not anymore. Now it's the new Featherstone house. And I'm Michael." He grinned at Jo. "Come up sometime. You can teach me Canadian."

Jo loved Michael's house with its bay windows, gingerbread trim and sunburst designs in the gables. It had a wonderful view, too. On clear days they could look south across the city, right to the edge, where it was framed by snow-capped mountains. "Those are the Olympics," Jo explained. "They're in Washington, in the United States, all the way across the strait. But they look close, don't they? And those hills —" She pointed to the range of low, purplish-blue hills in the west. "Those are the Sooke Hills. They're closer."

Michael showed her the upstairs, where the rooms had sloping ceilings. The bedrooms were at the back, but at the front was a study with an almost-secret cupboard. It was built into the papered wall so skilfully you hardly knew it was there.

"Have a look," Michael said. He handed her a flashlight.

Jo crawled inside. "Good hiding place. Have you stashed any treasures yet? Or found anything?" She shone the light along the sloping walls, hoping to find a scrawled message or a tunnel leading to another hidden cupboard.

"Not yet. I looked really closely, but couldn't find a thing."

"Wait a sec'. There *is* something here." In the far corner, the light caught a white edge just above the floor molding. Jo pulled on it, and scuttled back excitedly. "An envelope! Addressed to Miss Emily Burgess. Look at the postmark. December, 1932. That's twenty-five years ago."

"It's still sealed," Michael said. "Which means Emily Burgess never opened it."

"Maybe she never got it." Jo's eyes shone with the possibilities. "Maybe it's from someone her parents didn't like, so they hid it on her. Or maybe she hid it from her parents and forgot about it. Or maybe it's a romantic letter from a faraway place, but it got lost in the house —"

"It's not from faraway," Michael pointed out. "See? Postmarked Victoria. Open it."

"A Christmas card!" They admired the heavenly host of angels and read the greeting. It was ordinary enough. But on the blank side was a note. *Dearest Emily, Please let me explain. Your forgiveness means everything. Your loving friend, B.*

Jo pointed to a smudge of black ink. "She was crying when she wrote this."

"Maybe," Michael said. "Or maybe she was a messy writer."

"Maybe it wasn't a she. The loving friend could have been a he."

"They must have had a fight about something."

"And Emily got mad and didn't want to see B again."

"And B finally got up enough courage to apologize and beg forgiveness —"

"But Emily never got the card so she never knew, and they both died of broken hearts." Jo grinned, pleased with their scenario. "I do that all the time," she confessed. "Make up stories. Talk them out to myself. Everybody on the street thinks I'm —" She paused, searching for a word.

"Certifiable," said Michael.

Jo gave him a puzzled look.

"I collect words," he explained. "It's a hobby of mine."

At home the next day, Jo asked, "What's certifiable?"

Dad looked up from his fishing lures. "Me, if I don't get these hoochies untangled."

"Dad, seriously."

"Seriously insane. That's certifiable."

It fit. That's exactly what Wendy and Sharon would call her if they knew the word.

"Ca-razy!" Ian attacked her from behind with the

rubbery tentacles of a squid-like hoochie.

Jo ignored him. "Instead of supper, can we call it *tea*? It sounds more posh."

"Sounds more Michael, you mean," Ian put in.

"Ian, get lost! Can we, Mom?"

Mom had been enlisted to help untangle, and was draped in fishing line. "Sure, dear."

"A rose by any other name," said Dad.

"What?"

"Call me what you like, just don't call me late for supper."

"Oh, brother." Why couldn't she have a normal dad, someone who didn't make a corny joke every time he opened his mouth?

"Want to come fishing with us tomorrow?" he asked.

"Nope. Michael's coming for lunch. We're having potato salad and tuna burgers and cake. Michael says they have their big meal at noon, and tea around suppertime. But he wants to learn the Canadian way. Now I'm going up there for tea." She tossed a shiny lure at Ian. "See ya later, alligator."

"Jo, wait! Are you sure Mrs. Featherstone doesn't mind?"

"She invited me, Mom. She's making 'bubble and squeak' especially."

"Sounds like hamsters," said Ian.

"Well it's not, for your information. It's some kind of great English food with mashed potatoes and cabbage. Not a *Chatelaine* Meal of the Month, either. No offense, Mom."

"Don't wear out your welcome, that's all."

"With Michael? He's the best friend I've ever had."

"What about Mack?" said Dad.

"What about her?" Jo unhooked the fishing lure stuck in Mom's sleeve.

"You were so happy going to Willows Beach, we wondered —"

"Nothing happened. Mack's older, that's all."

"She was always older."

"I know, but . . . Oh, I don't know," Jo said. "It's different now."

6

The difference was Michael. For the two weeks before school started, they were inseparable. Sometimes Jo had tea at Michael's. Sometimes Michael had lunch at Jo's. He laughed the first time she offered him a cookie. "A *cookie*? Where I come from, they're biscuits."

Jo remembered her dad's comment. "A rose by any other name," she said.

"Shakespeare!" Michael took the cue and launched into the story of Romeo and Juliet.

"How do you know all that?"

"I'm naturally brilliant."

Jo groaned.

"All right, all right," said Michael. "I learned it in school. I was in grammar school last year, after I passed my Eleven Plus exams. We studied a bit of Shakespeare. And Latin, *ad nauseam*."

Jo was impressed.

He liked playing around on her piano, and quickly mastered "Chopsticks." Jo taught him "Heart and Soul" as a duet and he pounded the chords while she played the melody. Flicka, curled up by the soft pedal, thumped her tail in approval.

When Michael started picking out the melody of an Elvis Presley hit, Jo said, "Elvis can't even read music. When someone asked him what his range was, he thought they were talking about his ranch. When I told Wendy and Sharon they said, 'Yeah, so? What's your point?' They didn't even know range meant how high and how low you can sing. Can you believe it? Some people."

"Who's Sharon and Wendy?" Michael wondered.

"Nobody. Just a couple of girls from school."

Sometimes Jo and Michael worked on the fort they were creating in the woods behind Michael's house. Not a real fort with a roof and walls and windows, but a large area cut into the dense bushes, sheltered from the wind, but open to the sky. "This'll be brilliant for stargazing," Michael said. "And for satellite-watching, if ever a satellite gets launched. I have to start practicing, you see. Since I'm going to be an astrophysicist."

"I'm going to be a concert pianist," Jo said. "Or a writer."

"Certifiable," Michael teased.

The fort was shaded by oak trees. Sometimes they

ate lunch there, then spent the afternoons smoking licorice pipes or sucking on jawbreakers, comparing the layers of color until only a tiny seed remained.

Sometimes they read in the fort. Other times Jo took her leather-bound book and wrote stories. "I finished the one about Mack almost drowning at Willows Beach," she said. "Now I'm writing one about Emily Burgess. You know, the one we sort of made up together?"

"It's a mystery, then?"

"A *tragic* mystery. And a ghost story, all in one."

Sometimes they just sat and talked. Jo could spend all day with Michael and never get bored, not like she did with Sharon and Wendy. When she told him about the avalanche, he got out the atlas and helped her find the Selkirk Mountains and Rogers Pass, even the town of Revelstoke where her grandparents had lived.

Unlike Sharon and Wendy, Michael didn't laugh when Jo told him about the angel whispering in Grandad's ear. "Maybe that's what happened to you," he said. "Remember when we met? If you hadn't left the beach when you did, and caught that bus, and ended up at the store —"

"You're right! Except for one big difference. There wasn't a disaster."

"Oh, I don't know." He gave her a mischievous grin. "I met you, didn't I?"

Jo showed Michael the way to school, both the long way around and the shortcut through the woods. "I like biking through here in the spring when the wild-flowers are out. There's shooting stars and Easter lilies.

The path gets muddy in the winter though, and the pond overflows. But if it's cold enough, the pond freezes and we go skating."

"Aren't there any kids around here?" Michael asked as they passed a trio of new houses built on the edge of the woods.

"Some, but they're away on holidays." She hurried him past Wendy's house, hoping that she — or worse, her twin brother, Donny — wouldn't appear.

Sometimes Jo and Michael took the bus to the library. The route went along a narrow street lined with chestnut trees, past Mack's high school, then down a wide street with old-fashioned houses. Once downtown, the bus inched along the busy streets, stopping at each block.

They got off at the Metropolitan Five and Dime, then crossed over to the English Sweet Shop so Michael could buy pear drops for his mom. From there, it was a short walk to the library.

After signing out their books, they usually went to the Nut House for bags of caramel or licorice popcorn. Once they walked an extra block to the bus stop on Pandora Street, situated outside London Fish and Chips. There they bought an order of chips, sprinkled them with salt and vinegar, and wrapped them in newspaper to eat on the way home.

"Does it make you homesick?" Jo asked as the bus rumbled through the traffic. "Eating chips from London Fish and Chips?"

"This is home now," said Michael.

"You must miss your friends."

"I didn't have many friends."

"Me neither, except for Mack. *Real* friends, I mean. Until you came," Jo added shyly. She reached for another chip and said, "This is what Mack and I used to do. We'd go to the library, then buy chips to eat on the bus." A memory came to her, as sharp as the taste of malt vinegar. She realized that without planning to, she'd followed the saying Mack used to have taped to her wall — *To attract good fortune, share an old pleasure with a new friend.* She felt a warmth inside that had nothing to do with the steaming chips.

On Labor Day weekend, Jo's dad took Michael and Mr. Featherstone fishing.

"I caught my first fish!" Michael exclaimed when he and Jo met later. "A salmon! A two-pound coho! See this?" He spread the morning newspaper across his kitchen table, open to the sports page. "The King Fisherman Contest! See all the names? My name'll be there, with the weight of my fish and where I caught it. Crikey! A two-pound coho! So, do you want to go to the pictures tomorrow? To celebrate?"

Jo gave him a blank look.

"The pictures! Mum said it was all right, if your parents don't mind. There's an Alfred Hitchcock thriller, *The Man Who Knew Too Much*. It costs twenty-five cents but I've got enough —"

"Ohh! You mean a *movie*."

"Do you want to? It doesn't have to be Hitchcock." He flipped to the movie page. "There's *Tammy and the Bachelor*. And *Delicate Delinquent* starring Jerry Lewis."

"A teenage terror who scares nobody but himself," Jo read. "Hey! How about *Creature with the Atom Brain*? Aah, too bad. It's at the Tillicum Outdoor Theatre."

"*The Man Who Knew Too Much*, then? The heroine's name is Jo."

"Great!" she said.

Early next morning, Jo was outside picking cherry tomatoes when she spotted Mack in her back yard. "Hi!" she called cheerfully. "I haven't seen you for days."

Mack leaned over the fence, a bouquet of sweet peas in her hand. "I think we know why," she laughed. "How's Michael? I hear you're going to the movies with him this afternoon. Well? Don't leave me in suspense. He's nice, and he's got beautiful blue eyes."

Jo blushed. "He's OK."

"He's OK," Mack mimicked. "I want all the details. In what way is he OK?"

"I don't know! He's just — Michael."

"Don't worry, I'm only teasing. There's absolutely no reason why you have to tell me anything." Mack handed Jo some rose and lavender sweet peas. "Here. For your room."

Jo breathed in the sweet fragrance and placed the flowers in her basket. "How come you're not at the beach?" she asked. "Won't Alan be pining away?"

Mack smiled sadly. "Probably, but no more than me. He had to go on day shift for the rest of the summer. You know, his car-hop job at the drive-in? We haven't seen each other for two weeks. That's why I can't wait till school starts."

"So you haven't gone to the beach at all?" Jo asked. "I thought you were mad at me for leaving early that time."

"Oh, no! I haven't gone because I couldn't go, not without my beach buddy! And it didn't seem like you were interested, what with Michael and all. Anyway, I've been getting ready for school. My last year, can you believe it? I'll be a grad! By the way, is your parents' badminton club starting soon?"

"Next Friday."

"You want some company, you and Ian?"

"Sure!" Jo gave Mack a cherry tomato, then bit into one of her own. It glistened with the chill morning dew, but the taste was warm and bittersweet, like the end of summer.

7

Sharon didn't waste a minute. As soon as she got home from Guide Camp she phoned Jo, eager to find out about the new kid in the old Burgess house. "Wendy told me you're together all the time," she said in her annoying singsong voice. "Did you really go to the movies with him? What's his name? Michael? I didn't know you went out on dates."

"It wasn't a date." How did Wendy know? Had she been spying on them? The thought made Jo's stomach squirm.

"Did you go with a boy?" Sharon prodded. "Without your parents? And sit beside him? And did he pay?"

"Yeah, but —"

"That makes it a date!" Sharon squealed. "You are so lucky! Do you want to come to my house after supper? Wendy and Diane are coming. So's Marilyn."

"I can't. I'm going to my grandma's."

"I bet! You've probably got another date with Michael. What are you wearing tomorrow? I got a new pleated skirt, same as Wendy's, only mine's blue and hers is green. And it's reversible! Did you hear Mr. West's the vice-principal? He's teaching grade seven so maybe we'll be in his class again, do you think? Do you want to walk with me and Wendy?"

Jo answered the questions, but the whole time her mind was on Michael. *Was* it a date?

No! He was just her best friend, that's all.

On the other hand, he was a boy. That's why she'd come home in agony, desperately needing to go to the bathroom. She couldn't get up to go in the middle of the movie, she just couldn't — he would have known! Besides, the movie was too exciting. And after it was over, when Michael said, "Hang on, I'm going to the Gents'," she *had* to wait, because what if he came out and couldn't find her? Well, she'd learned one lesson. Next time, she wouldn't order a large drink. And next time —

"*Jo!* Are you listening or what?"

"Sorry. What did you say?"

"What I said was, who do you think Michael will have to shark?"

Jo swallowed hard. "Michael?"

"Come on, Jo," Sharon laughed. "*You* know, every-body knows. It's a school tradition. New kids always have to shark somebody. It's how they get accepted."

"Michael's not like that. He doesn't care about being accepted."

"We'll see." Sharon's voice gleamed with smugness.

The first day of school always felt like a piano exam. Jo got up an hour early and thumped a few chords to scare away the jitters.

It didn't work.

She put on her new white blouse, red corduroy jumper and saddle shoes, then brushed her hair and tied it in a ponytail. She held up a mirror and examined her profile, first right, then left. She checked the back view. She practiced smiling.

"You look lovely, dear," Mom said when she sat down for breakfast. "Bright as a new coat of paint."

Jo picked at a piece of toast. "Does my hair look all right?"

"Just *lovely*," said Ian.

She shot him a look and went back to her room, leaving the toast unfinished.

Everything was laid out, ready to go. Exercise books, dictionary, a box of crayons and a bottle of white paste, with brush. Watercolor paints, drawing portfolio, ruler with a metal edge. The Black Magic chocolate box was filled with HB and BB pencils, a Pink Pearl eraser, a box of nibs and a red penholder.

Jo loved the smell of new school supplies. Crisp pages to be filled, pencils to be sharpened, pen nibs to dip into ink and write stories. A whole year stretched ahead, filled with possibilities. And this year, for the first time, she'd be starting out with her own best friend.

Her stomach jumped. What if Michael wasn't in her class? What if Sharon or Wendy said something stupid? What if Wendy and her idiot brother, Donny, *had* been spying on them?

Well, so what? It wasn't as if she had anything to hide.

Still . . .

Maybe she should take Michael to Sharon's so they could all walk together, instead of her and Michael riding their bikes. Maybe she should have introduced him to other grade sevens in the neighborhood, instead of keeping him to herself.

Too late now. He'd be here any minute. And to be honest, there was another reason Jo hadn't wanted him to meet the others. If Michael was her friend, there was a good chance she wouldn't be the one to get sharked.

Sharking. No one remembered when the tradition started, or where the expression came from. Only that it had nothing to do with fish.

While she was waiting, Jo looked up *shark* in her dictionary. *A rapacious crafty person who preys upon others through usury, extortion or trickery.* Most of that didn't fit, but *crafty* and *preys upon* were getting close.

Shark was a verb, too, she discovered. *To gather hastily.* That fit the tradition of sharking. But nowhere did her dictionary describe how frightening it was, how humiliating, and worst of all, how unavoidable — if you were the one chosen.

"It's not so bad," Sharon had once told her. "And it doesn't hurt."

Wendy had offered some advice. "If it ever happens to you, just yell and scream a lot. Act really scared, but let them have what they want. Usually it's some little thing, like a shoe, or a scarf or something. Mostly all they want is to scare you. It's the pounce they like, that's what Donny told me. The pounce and grab."

Jo shuddered. The boys might not even *want* Michael as a sharker. It wasn't like it was decided or anything. Maybe there was an unwritten rule saying a person didn't have to do it if he came from England.

She heard a knock on the front door, followed by Mom's voice. "Jo, are you ready? Michael's here."

"Coming!" Jo closed her dictionary, gathered up her school supplies and gave her appearance one final check. She kissed her mother good-bye, then hurried outside.

On the way to school, she remembered that the new kid had to pass some kind of test first, to see if he was worthy of being a sharker. A happy thought came to mind — Michael might fail. Better yet, he might not care enough to try.

8

It started as soon as they rode onto the playground. "Hey, everybody!" Gil called out. "Donny was right! Jo's got a boyfriend!" A group of boys swaggered over to the bike racks. Sharon and Wendy, in reversible skirts and matching twin sweater sets, snickered in the background.

Jo pushed past Gil and locked up her bike. "Just ignore them, Michael."

"Hey, kid." Gil stabbed Michael's chest with a pudgy finger. "Where ya from?"

"Elephant and Castle. It's an area in London, England."

Jo groaned inwardly and tried to hurry him along.

"How come you're carrying a purse?" said Bob.

"It's for my books. And it's not a purse, actually. It's a satchel. From the Latin *saccellus*, meaning sack."

"Mich-*ael!*"

Gil gave a hoot and stabbed Michael again. "What's your name?"

"Michael Featherstone. What's yours?"

"Featherstone? Thought it was Freckles!"

"String Bean's more like it," Donny laughed. "No — *Limey* Bean, get it?"

Jo glared. "Why don't you morons shut up? Come on, Michael." She led him to the front of the school where kids were gathering in groups. "We won't have to wait long. Our grade gets called first."

She stood alone with Michael, like a small island. Sharon, Wendy and the other grade seven girls drifted by, raising their eyebrows, giving knowing smiles. What they thought they knew, Jo couldn't imagine. Then they stood in a huddle, whispering and giggling, casting more knowing looks over their shoulders.

The boys stood in a separate group, signing the cast on Doug's arm. "Think I'll take a look," Michael said. "I had a broken ulna once. You know the ulna? It's one of the bones on your forearm."

Jo said, "Believe me, they won't care." But Michael was already sauntering over to the boys.

Right away, the girls circled in. "Is he weird, or what? Why is he wearing those ugly pants?"

"At least they're long." Jo glanced at Michael's gray flannels. "In England, boys wear short pants to school until they're fourteen."

"Get a load of his blazer," Marilyn said. "And

57

his tie. What about that, Jo?"

Thank heavens she'd persuaded him not to wear his grammar school cap. "It's only because it's the first day," she said. "He wanted — " She didn't have time to finish. Her stomach gave another jump as the principal raised a megaphone and began calling out the names.

Jo was pleased to have Mr. West again.

Once everyone had taken their seats, he grinned at the familiar faces and said, "I know you thought you'd seen the last of me, but *c'est la vie*. I'm looking forward to the best year ever."

"Does that mean longer recess?" Gil asked.

Mr. West laughed and shook his head. "Oh, Gil. Always the joker."

Instead of assigning the usual "What I Did During the Summer Holidays," Mr. West wanted to try something new. He held up a battered cork boot and said, "This is a souvenir of how I spent my summer. Logging! You might have a souvenir, too. Maybe it's a cast, from when you fell out of a tree." Everyone laughed as Doug brandished his plaster-wrapped arm. "Maybe it's a feeling you want to keep, to remember your last summer as elementary school kids. Next year — if you pass — it's junior high." He paused to let that sink in. "Now, I'm going to draw names from this boot, and you're going to interview your partner. Find out the best and worst thing that happened during their summer. Then report back to the class."

Donny raised his hand. "Is it going to be separate, sir? Boys and girls?"

"How many boots do you see?" said Mr. West.

"One, but —"

"We're all in this class together. Boys and girls. So boys may end up with a girl partner and vice versa."

Some of the boys pulled faces. Sharon and Wendy looked disgusted, but Jo figured they were secretly pleased.

"One more thing," Mr. West said. "We're playing by Poker Face Rules. If you don't like your partner you do *not* show it in any way, shape or form. And if your partner turns out to be the greatest thing since cornflakes, you don't show that either. No reaction, that's the Poker Face Rules." One by one he drew the names.

For the third time within an hour, Jo felt sick. What was best about her summer? Michael. But she couldn't embarrass him by saying it in front of the class. And who would she be paired with? Not Gil — oh please, not him.

"Now, right inside the toe . . ." Mr. West rummaged around and pulled out two names. "Jo and Bob."

Oh, well. Could be worse.

They were given five minutes to interview their partners, then everyone returned to their desks to hear the presentations. As luck would have it, Jo was first to speak.

She stood up, stomach churning, her face as red as her jumper. "This is my friend Bob," she said, beginning as Mr. West had instructed them. "He spent the summer at his family's cabin. The worst thing was when he lost a big salmon and —"

"Shark," Bob interrupted.

"That's not what you said before!" Jo shouted over the laughter, quickly squelched by a glare from Mr. West. What did Bob go and say "shark" for? Was it some kind of message? She glanced around to see if the boys were exchanging meaningful looks, but they were too busy holding back their laughter. She finished in a rush. "And the best thing was seeing a bunch of killer whales."

"Pod," Bob corrected.

"OK, then. Pod." She sat down, breathless, while the class followed the West Rule of Applauding. Like her piano exam, it felt good once it was over. But why "shark"? Had the boys already picked her as the target? No. It was way too soon. Michael hadn't even had the test.

She turned her attention to Bob's presentation. "The worst thing about Jo's summer . . ." He paused. "There wasn't a worst thing. But the best thing was, she found out she got First Class Honors in her grade five piano exam."

Mr. West smiled his congratulations and everyone clapped. Jo felt the clapping was for her as much as for Bob, although her classmates were probably disappointed nothing bad had happened. What was the worst thing about her summer? Stupid Alan showing up at the beach and gushing over Mack. But she couldn't mention that. She should have invented something, like a midnight encounter with the ghost of Emily Burgess.

When it was Michael's turn, Jo felt sick all over again. Some kids were stuffing fists in their mouths to keep from giggling. Sharon looked annoyed. Nobody seemed to care what Michael said about her. They only wanted to hear his Englishy way of saying it.

"And that," he concluded, "was the most transcendental, unparagoned event of her summer."

Jo watched Mr. West's gray eyes turn into the steelie boulders of Ian's marble collection. "What?"

Still following the Poker Face Rules, Michael repeated, "The most transcendental, unparagoned —"

"Explain, please."

"It means best, sir."

"I know perfectly well what it means, young man. I want to know why you're making a mockery of this exercise."

"I didn't mean to, sir. Sharon was so happy about her summer I needed a bigger word than best."

"He collects words," Jo burst out. "It's like a hobby. He does it all the time."

"Thank you, Jo, for enlightening us." He turned back to Michael. "Enlightening means clearing things up. You knew that, no doubt."

"Yes, sir."

"I can see we're going to have a most interesting year." He eyeballed Michael for another few seconds, then looked away. "All right, now. Are there any presentations left?"

"Me, sir," Sharon said. "This is my friend Michael."

Everyone giggled.

"He's from London, England, and lives a block away from me."

More giggling.

"The worst thing that happened was he tried a mixture of Worse — Wooster . . ." She looked to Michael for help.

"Worcestershire," he said.

"Right. A mixture of that sauce and some vinegar, and he drank it to get rid of his freckles but it made them multiply instead."

The class burst out laughing. Mr. West glared.

"That's what he said, sir!" Sharon exclaimed. "Honest! And the best thing was, he got to shoot his very own gun that his grandfather left him, and after weeks of practicing he could shoot the bull's eye!" She sat down to enthusiastic applause.

Jo was puzzled. Michael, shooting a gun? He had never mentioned a gun, but it must be important. Why else would he tell the whole class? Unless it was something he made up to impress everybody. *That* she could understand.

For years she'd told everyone that her dad had been a hero in the Second World War and had the medals to prove it. No, she couldn't bring them to school, not even on Remembrance Day, because they were too valuable. Her mother had been a Hollywood movie star before she married the famous war hero. And he wasn't an ordinary electrician like everyone thought, but an undercover spy in disguise.

In grade two, when nobody had anything interesting for Show and Tell, Jo told the class about her new baby sister and how she'd been born in a taxi on the way to the hospital. That evening, her teacher had phoned Jo's mother to congratulate her, much to Mom's surprise.

So Jo understood how stories could be used to get attention, even to gain status. Until you were found out. Or unless nobody cared.

But Gil and the other boys cared. As soon as they were dismissed they bombarded Michael with questions about the gun. Where did he get it? When? What kind? What size bullets? Trouble was, they didn't understand half the answers.

Jo asked about it on the way home. "Is it really true? Why didn't you tell me? It's not a secret, is it? How come I never saw you shooting?"

"Whoa! Yes, it's true, it's not important, it's not a secret, and I haven't shot it since we moved here. All right?"

"All right! Don't get your knickers in a knot," she said, using Mrs. Featherstone's expression. "I do have one more question. Stop groaning, it's not about the gun. What *was* the best thing that happened to Sharon? I can't remember what you said."

"She got a new Elvis Presley record."

Jo laughed. "No wonder you needed a bigger word than best."

All week the boys hammered away about the gun. It wasn't enough that Michael told them it was a Webley six-shot revolver, made in England, or that it fired .38 Smith and Wesson cartridges. They didn't care that it had been issued to his grandfather by the Royal Air Force during the Second World War. They weren't satisfied when he brought rubbings of the letters RAF, stamped on the plate on the right hand side of the revolver. They wanted to see it.

"Where's your gun, Featherstone?" Gil persisted. "Prove you've got one, why doncha? Show us after school."

"Too much homework, sorry."

"Saturday, then."

"I'm not allowed to have anyone over."

"How come Jo's always over? Have you shown her your gun?"

Michael didn't answer.

"You're full of it, Limey. You don't have a gun."

"He does too!" Jo said. "I even fired it, so there!"

Nobody believed her. "You'd say anything, Gillespie. You always were a liar."

"Yeah," Donny said. "You wouldn't know which end to shoot. Betcha can't tell the pointy end from the butt!"

The boys found this hilarious. Jo gave them a how-pathetic look and said, "So funny I forgot to laugh."

When the boys weren't pestering Michael about the gun, they were ridiculing his appearance. "Hey, Featherstone, how come your arms are so long? How come you're so skinny? Ever tried pinning your ears back? How about those freckles?"

"Yeah, Featherstone. Try some more Worser Sauce."

"Try choking on it!"

When the buzzer went, the taunts followed them into the school. "Shut up!" Jo shouted over her shoulder.

"Oooh!" They froze in mock horror.

"Better run for it, guys," Doug said. "Feather-weight's siccing Jo on us."

"Hey, Feathers. Heard any big words lately?"

"What about this big gun of yours, huh? Or was that just a bunch of bull-ony?"

"Hey, Limey, turn around! We're talking to Y-O-U!"

Without turning, Michael hung up his coat and walked to his desk.

"How do you do it?" Jo whispered.

"Poker Face Rules," said Michael.

"Keep it up!" And maybe, Jo added silently, they'll give up and leave you alone.

A few days later, Jo and Michael were in the fort enjoying an Indian Summer Saturday. "So do you?" Jo asked.

Michael raised his eyebrows. "Do I what?"

"Have a gun? It's OK if you don't. I used to make up stories all the time. I thought it would make me more interesting."

"I've already told you it's true. But I wish I'd never mentioned it."

"Why don't you let them see it? Then they'd shut up."

"Seeing it wouldn't be enough."

She finished her "toad in the hole" sausage and washed it down with a glass of orange Freshie. "I guess not," she said. "Not for those morons. But it would be enough for me."

So after lunch they went to the upstairs study. Michael crawled inside the almost-secret cupboard and came back with a box. He opened it and lifted out the Webley. "Don't worry, it's not loaded. Dad keeps the cartridges locked in the kitchen sideboard." He handed it to her. "Careful, it's heavy."

It was much heavier than she'd expected. Way too heavy to twirl around her finger like the cowboys on TV did.

"Here's the RAF marking." Michael pointed it out. "And see the little arrow? That's stamped on there to show it's British Armed Forces Property. Not anymore though. That's why there's an X over the shaft of the arrow."

"How do you load it?"

He pressed a lever on the left-hand side, grabbed the end of the barrel and pulled down. "You put the cartridges in the cylinder, pointed end first. Then push up on the barrel. It closes and locks." He clicked it back into place. "Try aiming."

Jo lifted it with both hands, closed one eye, and sighted along the barrel. "It's different from the guns in the westerns," she said. "There isn't one of those things you pull back on."

"You cock this kind with the trigger," Michael explained. "Use your index finger and pull back hard. That releases the hammer, and then it fires. It's a spring mechanism. You see —"

"Never mind, Michael. I don't have to know every-thing about it." She needed both index fingers to pull the trigger. "Ready, aim, fire!"

Click.

A bullet would have shattered the window. And if she'd been aiming in a different direction?

"Here, Michael. I've seen it." Even after she gave it back, her hands were shaking.

9

On Monday after school, the boys were waiting at the bike racks. "Hey, Featherstone, how come you hang around with Jo? Whaddya do in the woods behind your place? Play fairy games? Is that why you hang around girls?"

"Shut up!" Jo pulled her bike from the racks and turned it sharply, grazing Donny's knee with the front wheel.

"Watch it!" he yelled.

"Get out of our way."

"Go ahead and make me." The boys circled in, laughing unpleasantly.

"Yeah, Jo," Gil said. "Let's see you do the fighting for your fairy boyfriend."

Without warning, Michael shoved his bike straight at Gil. The boy was so surprised he jumped aside. But before Michael could get away, Bob and Donny moved in and blocked him.

"What now, fairy?" Gil pressed his fist hard under Michael's chin. "Fight your way outta this one, why doncha?"

A crowd had gathered, making encouraging noises in the background. "Yeah! You show him!" someone called out, but whether he was referring to Michael or Gil, Jo couldn't say.

"Come on, fairy," Donny snarled. He dug Michael in the ribs with an elbow.

"Fairies don't fight." Michael's voice sounded tight and gravelly, but he kept speaking in spite of the pressure on his throat. "Fairies fly away or vanish or use their magic wands to turn bullies like you into toads. I can't do any of those things so *ipso facto* I'm not a fairy. I'm a *Homo sapiens*, like you. *Mankind* is what the term refers to."

"Huh?"

"Didn't you know you were a *Homo sapiens?*" In one quick movement his hand shot up, grasped Gil's wrist and yanked it away from his throat. "You are, too," he said, turning to Bob and Donny. "You should thank me for improving your vocabulary."

Gil spat on the ground. "Come on, guys. This kid's a wacko." They swaggered off.

Jo turned to Michael. "*Ipso fatso?* You're lucky he didn't beat your head in."

The next morning, Jo entered the classroom to find everyone peering excitedly out the window. "What happened?" she asked.

"Jo to the rescue," Donny laughed. "Maybe she'll get it."

"Get what?"

"My satchel," Michael explained. "Gil and Donny were tossing it around, and Donny threw it out the window. Complete with my homework."

"So? Go outside and get it."

"He can't," Sharon said. "It landed on that ledge below the window. See? It's too far to lean out."

Everyone had a comment or suggestion.

"He'll have to wait for the janitor."

"Mr. West could climb up a ladder."

"West better not find out. He'll kill you, Donny."

"Get the yardstick and knock it off, why doncha?"

"It won't reach, stupid!"

Suddenly Wendy yelled, "Michael, don't! You'll get killed!"

But Michael was already lowering himself to the ledge. "Don't worry. It's fairly wide." His classmates cheered as he reached the ledge and stooped to pick up his satchel. "Rather pleasant, actually." He grinned up at them. "Except for the wind. Anyone care to hand me my blazer? Perhaps I'll spend the morning out here." He sat down and swung his legs over the edge. "Smashing view from the second floor."

"Enjoy it!" Bob sang, and slammed the window shut.

"You idiot!" Sharon pushed him out of the way

and was about to open the window when someone yelled, "Teacher!"

In seconds, they were in their desks, staring straight ahead. After the Bible reading and Lord's Prayer, Mr. West said, "Writing books out. Your handwriting exercise is on the board."

"But sir —" Jo raised her hand.

"Not now. Do as you're told."

"But —" Wendy tried again.

"Not now!" He slammed a pile of books on his desk and began to mark.

What was in *his* cornflakes? Jo wondered. For a while there were no sounds except for the dipping of pens in inkwells, and the scratch-scratch of nibs on paper. But beyond the scratching, her ears picked up something else. A faint tapping, like raindrops. Only these raindrops were hitting the window pane to the rhythm of "O Canada!"

Mr. West heard it too. "What's going on?" He leapt to his feet, then stopped abruptly. "What the —?"

"It's Michael!" said Jo.

"I can see that!"

The sight of Michael's face, seemingly disembodied and floating two storeys above the ground, was too much. The whole class erupted.

"Stop it at once!" Mr. West roared.

Michael knocked on the window. "Crikey, sir! Please let me in. It's beastly cold."

Mr. West threw up the sash and extended a hand.

"Thank you, sir," Michael said as he climbed back in. "Whew!" He walked to his desk, took his books out of his satchel and nonchalantly picked up his pen.

"Whew?" Mr. West repeated. "That's the best you can do?"

"I'm speechless, sir. Sorry."

"You're going to be a lot sorrier. What, may I ask, were you doing on that ledge?"

"Getting my satchel, sir."

Mr. West's mouth tightened in a thin line. "What was your satchel doing on the ledge?"

The whole class held its breath.

"Well?" shouted Mr. West. "Get on with it!"

"It landed there."

"HOW?" The word echoed like a gunshot. Jo's heart pounded, the way it had in the Hitchcock movie. All they needed now was a crash of cymbals.

"I was leaning out the window," Michael said calmly. "To see if I'd locked my bike. And the satchel slipped out of my hands. That's all. Except for the window not staying open. When I was about to start back in, it fell shut. It could have fallen on my fingers. It should be repaired, sir."

Mr. West's eyes roved around the classroom. "So it was all your doing, Michael? No one helped you out with this little adventure?"

"No, sir."

For a long moment, the only sound was the release of held-in breath.

"Week's detention," Mr. West said sternly. His eyes took another slow tour of the room. They rested on Gil, moved on to Donny, stopped at Bob, and returned to Michael. No one said a word.

And Jo knew, in the pit of her stomach, that Michael had passed the test.

All that remained was the sharking.

10

It wasn't long before Michael was part of the group. Jo didn't spend half as much time with him as she used to, although they still biked to school together and saw each other in class. They also talked on the phone practically every night, and met in the fort most Saturday mornings.

One Saturday, Jo arrived with a basket of shiny red apples. "These are from our tree," she said. She took a bite. "They're delicious."

"Thought they were MacIntosh."

"Very funny." She took another bite. "Hard on the outside, sweet and juicy inside. They're not all for you — your parents can have some, too. So do you want to do something after lunch?"

Michael polished an apple with the front of his shirt. "Thought you went to your grandparents' after lunch."

"Usually. But I don't have to."

"Sorry, then." Between bites, he said, "Saturday afternoons I'm going to the arena. Didn't I tell you? Bob's teaching me to skate. Once I start my paper round — route, I mean — I'll be able to buy my own skates. Did you know a carrier can earn between twenty-five and forty-five dollars a month?"

"Only if you're a boy," Jo mumbled. Skating every Saturday? Why couldn't he wait till the pond froze? She could teach him to skate.

"And once I skate well enough," Michael continued, "I'll be able to play hockey. Then I'll feel like a real Canadian."

"Tomorrow, then? Want to go biking somewhere?"

"Can't. Dad says Sundays are beach days, as long as the weather's good. Last week we went to Witty's Lagoon, just outside Victoria. Have you been there?"

Jo crunched on her apple. "Lots of times."

"A smashing beach, especially when the tide's out. Miles and miles of sand. I tried to estimate the number of grains, actually. One quintillion on an average beach. That's a one followed by thirty zeros. Only thing is, I'm not sure if Witty's is an average beach. What do you think?"

"Why don't you ask Gil or Donny? Or brilliant Bob? And I suppose they've been having a great time with that stupid gun of yours. I can just hear it." Imitating Michael's accent, she drawled, "Oh Gil, let

74

me help you load it. Oh, Bob! You've hit the target. Jolly good, old chap."

"Don't be nasty!" Michael snapped. "They're nice, once you get to know them. All that bullying stuff was just an act. And stop being so possessive."

Possessive? She finished her apple and chucked the core hard into the bushes, wishing she'd had the courage to aim at Michael's snotty English head.

"Look, Jo," he continued. "There's certain things I like to talk to you about. Like the grains of sand. The others wouldn't know or care, but you . . . Different friends for different times, you know?"

"And I'm Saturday morning's friend," Jo muttered.

"What?"

"Never mind." Before she left, she bit into another apple to drive away the sour taste in her mouth.

She'd been right, the day of the ledge. After Michael's week of detentions, the boys asked him to play basketball and urged him to try out for the school team. He was tall. And a good player. Besides, they were tired of picking on him. What do you do with someone who never tells, who twists your words and throws them back in your face, who turns your pranks to his advantage and comes out a hero? Sometimes Jo caught herself wishing Michael *had* told after the ledge prank. Then he would still be an outsider.

The thought made her ashamed. At the same time, she meant it. Partly because of the sharking and her fear of being chosen. And partly because Michael was right. She was possessive. She wanted to keep him to herself.

Thank heavens for Mack. Every Friday night, Jo's parents went to their badminton club, then to a get-together with friends. Mack came over as promised, not to babysit but to keep Jo and Ian company. She didn't have to stay until the Gillespies came home — well past midnight — but she did, even though Jo and Ian were asleep by ten. When Ian asked why, Mack said, "Your TV's better than ours. And my parents pull the plug right after the evening news. This way I get to watch what I want."

She brought her usual assortment of games, puzzles and treats, along with her collection of Elvis records.

"Wouldn't you rather be with Alan?" Jo asked one night. Ian was in his room in the basement sorting marbles, and Mack was cleaning up in a Monopoly game. Jo had once again landed in jail.

"To tell you the truth, yes," said Mack. "But he's at work. Car-hopping every weekend."

"This isn't about Alan, but I was wondering . . ." Jo paused, then hurried on. "Did they have sharking when you were in grade seven?"

Mack looked up from her Boardwalk hotels. "What?" she laughed. "They're still doing that?"

"I think Michael has to do it."

"Don't worry," Mack said. "Honestly. The boys think it's so important. But think about it. What's the big deal? So there's about six boys and they corner somebody and the new kid has to rip something off. Like it proves something? Big act of courage."

"But what about the person that gets sharked? Did you?"

"Yup, but I gave worse than I got. There's no way those creeps were taking anything of mine without permission. But you know what the worst part was? Not knowing when it was going to happen. Once you've been picked, you have to wait. Could be two days or two months. They could get you one morning on the way to school, or one night coming home, or at recess on the playground — not usually at school, though. But maybe the rules have changed. Different rules for different times."

Her words reminded Jo of Michael. "Do you think you can have different friends for different times? Like days of the week?"

"Well . . ." Mack absently fingered the row of houses on Park Place. "There's fair-weather friends. They're loyal only when it pleases them, when things are going right. The only days-of-the-week stuff I know about are those boxed sets of panties. You know, the don't-wear-the-ones-marked-Friday-on-Saturday kind? Friends don't come in boxed sets. Not good friends, the ones you would die for. Hey, cheer up! If Michael has to shark someone — "

"How do they pick?"

"Names on crumpled-up bits of paper. Where do you think I got my Choose Day idea? If you're picked, they give you a sign. Like a drawing of a shark, or something equally subtle."

"But sometimes — "

"Yeah, sometimes they stack the deck. But you're Michael's friend. He wouldn't hurt you. And anyway, chances are it won't be you, right? Feel better?" She handed Jo the dice. "Here. Take an extra turn and get out of jail."

Jo grinned. Thank heavens for Mack.

On the last Friday in September, Jo woke to a tapping sound. Not an ordinary tapping, but a message kind of tapping. She heard it a second time. Then the front door opened.

It wasn't her parents. They always walked right in. It had to be Mack. Letting someone else in.

Jo lay in bed not breathing and listened. She heard whispers, and a rustling sound. Soft laughter, and footsteps going into the living room. She crept out of bed and cautiously opened the door. Funny, she didn't remember closing it. And the hall was unexpectedly dark.

Through the roaring in her ears she heard more whispers and rustlings, followed by the groan of the couch springs. Her stomach jumped. Whatever was going on wasn't supposed to be going on. What should she do? Go and look? What if she saw something she wasn't meant to see? Would she tell her parents?

No. Better go back to bed and pretend she hadn't heard a thing.

She burrowed under the covers and was almost asleep when she remembered the phone calls. Every Friday night someone had phoned and asked for Mr. Gillespie. When Jo offered to take a message, the caller always said, "No, thanks," and hung up. So someone wanted her dad; they'd call back the next day. So the voice was familiar; why wouldn't it be, when she'd heard it four Fridays in a row? She hadn't given it a second thought.

Now it hit her. The voice was familiar because she'd heard it all summer at Willows Beach. Without having to look, she knew a '51 Chevy was parked two blocks away. And something told her this wasn't the first Friday night Alan had tapped on the door.

Sometime later, she heard a whisper. "Jo, are you awake?"

She opened her eyes to find Mack sitting on the edge of the bed. The door was open and the hall light was on, the way it was supposed to be.

"I've got a present for you." Mack unfastened her pearl drop earrings and tucked them in Jo's hand.

The pearls felt warm. Jo had always loved them, the way they shimmered in the light. "Why?"

Mack smiled. "I just want you to have them, OK?"

"Uh-huh," Jo said sleepily. "G'night."

When she woke the next morning, she was surprised to find the earrings under her pillow. Then she remembered. Instead of being pleased, she felt miserable. Mack must have heard her get up. Was this her way of keeping Jo quiet? Give a present, walk away. Secrets kept. No questions asked.

The pearls looked flat and cold. Somehow, they had lost their shine.

11

Jo hadn't seen much of Sharon and Wendy since school started. She knew they often went to Wendy's after school to listen to records or watch the dance show "American Bandstand." Wendy had invited Jo a couple of times, but she always said she had to go home and practice the piano.

On Monday, she was gathering her things in the cloakroom when Wendy invited her again. "Sorry," Jo said. "I have to practice."

"Practice, shmactice!" Sharon grabbed her coat from the hook and flung it over her shoulders. "You should quit piano, like I did. All those scales? Yuck! And Block? Double yuck."

"I think you mean Bach," Jo said.

"Who cares. Why don't you learn to play Elvis?"

"Ha!" Wendy gave a snort. "She's never heard of Elvis."

"Have too!" Jo declared hotly. "Bet I know more about Elvis than you do."

"Ooh!" The girls looked at each other with raised eyebrows. "Really? Like what?" Marilyn and Diane moved across the cloakroom to listen.

"Well, for one thing he had a twin brother who died at birth. And his middle name is Aaron and he doesn't drink or smoke. And when Mack was in Toronto she went to his concert at Maple Leaf Gardens. She's got all his records and we listen to them all the time. And I can play Elvis on the piano," she added proudly. "I can play 'Don't be Cruel' and 'Love Me Tender.'"

"Cool!" Wendy gave her an admiring smile.

"Hey, Jo," Sharon said, "I've got a great idea. Do you want to come to my pajama party on Saturday? All you have to do is bring a sleeping bag, a pillow and something to eat. And magazines if you've got any, and records. *Elvis* records 'cause it's an Elvis pajama party."

"I don't have any," Jo said.

"Then borrow Mack's! Will you, Jo? Please?"

"Sure!" Jo smiled happily. So what if she didn't worship Elvis like the others? She could fake it if she had to. The important thing was the pajama party. She'd never been to one before.

She walked outside with the girls and joined in the chatter of who was bringing what. She waved good-bye at the bike racks and rode home, feeling happier than she had in ages.

"Here, boy! Good dog!"

"Come on, atta boy!"

The voices of Ian and his friend Wayne drifted down the hall.

"What's going on, Flick?" Jo dropped her books at the front door and gave Flicka the aren't-you-glad-I'm-home scratch behind the ear. "Has Ian found a stray puppy? Eh, girl?"

No such luck. She walked into the kitchen to find the boys rolling their yoyos across the linoleum.

"See, Jo? We can do Walk the Dog. Wanna try?" Ian gave his yoyo a slight tug and returned it to his hand.

"Maybe later. Mom, can I go to Sharon's on Saturday night?"

"Watch us do Around the World, Mom."

"Not in here, you don't. You'll put someone's eye out."

"Can I, Mom? It's a pajama party," Jo said.

"It's for the Parsley Club. For Elvis the Pelvis fans." Ian and Wayne hooted with laughter.

Jo ignored them. "It's for Sharon's friends. So can I?"

"What?" Mom eyed the yoyos nervously.

"Don't worry," Ian said. "This is just the Sleeper. Hey, Wayne! Can you do a four-second Sleeper?"

"Sure, watch."

"*Mom!* The pajama party! Aren't you listening?"

"Of course, dear. Anything you need to take?"

"Elvis records. And potato chips."

"Why the sudden interest in Elvis?"

"*Everybody's* interested in Elvis." And what else have I got to do? Jo wondered silently. Michael's so tied up with basketball and hockey games and stupid skating he hardly even knows I exist. As for Mack . . .

"Everybody who's anybody, you mean?"

"No. I mean . . . Oh, I don't know."

"Maybe Mack will lend you some records. She seems to be the expert in that department."

"Yeah." Since Friday night, Jo had been unable to get Mack out of her mind. She thought of her whenever the phone rang. Whenever someone knocked on the door. Whenever she saw the pearl earrings nestled in her jewel case. And every time she felt uneasy.

Without warning, she blurted out, "Mom, I don't want Mack to come on Friday nights anymore. Ian and I are old enough, and we don't need her for company."

"Fine with me. How about you, Ian?"

"Yeah, I'm sick of her records. Hey, Wayne. Let's go outside and try the Orbit Launch."

"OK, but you need at least a six-second Sleeper for that one."

"Ea-sy!"

Mom watched them go out the back door and laughed. "Orbit Launch! What I need is a cup of tea. Join me?" She poured Jo a cup and said, "I'll let Mack know, then. Unless you want to?"

"No, that's OK." Jo sipped her tea, relieved. But mingled with the relief was a surprising sense of loss.

"So! I've turned you into a Presley addict." Mack handed Jo a pile of records, a stack of *Photoplays* and a *True Confessions* magazine. "Take care of these, and don't let anyone else touch the records. Promise?"

"I'll guard them with my life."

"You don't have to go that far. Just don't get them scratched." She showed Jo to the door. "Too bad about Friday nights. You don't want the company, eh? Guess you're all grown up now."

Jo didn't say anything. She gave Mack a small smile and walked home, troubled by the same uneasy feeling she'd had before. Maybe she'd dreamed the whole thing. Or imagined it as a story. Maybe Mack had given her the earrings because she was what she'd always been — a nice person. A friend.

Jo wondered why she didn't come right out and talk about it with Mack. Say, "The other night I thought I heard . . ." then watch Mack's reaction. That's what a grown-up person would do.

"You're all grown up." Hardly. *Groan* up was more like it. Things were supposed to get easier when you got older. Instead, they got harder. And much more confusing.

12

Saturday!

Jo tried to speed up the day by reading, practic-ing, working on a story. She vacuumed the living room and made seven-minute frosting for Mom's chocolate cake. The newspaper headline caught her attention — *Russian-Fired Satellite Circles in Space*. She spent several minutes reading about the launching that astonished the world. Sputnik! She phoned Michael to see if he'd heard the news, but he wasn't home.

The hours dragged — through early morning showers, wind gusting in the afternoon, and a typical October downpour in the evening.

Finally, it was time. Jo packed her things, rolled up

the musty sleeping bag, grabbed an umbrella, and headed up the hill. On the way, she passed Michael's house and couldn't resist calling through the rain, "Who needs you, Michael? I'm going to Sharon's, so there!"

Before long, there were five girls in Sharon's basement, sprawled on pillows in the rec room, munching chips and French onion dip. Lights from the orphanage across the street shone hazily through the window.

"Hey, Jo," Sharon said, "remember when you told everybody you came from that orphanage?"

Jo's face reddened.

"You said you escaped one night after getting beaten with a leather strap, and Mr. and Mrs. Gillespie found you under their weeping willow tree."

"Half dead," Diane added.

"And they decided to adopt you."

"Nobody believed you," Sharon said, "but we all pretended we did. Then there was that story about the hanging tree, remember?"

Marilyn frowned. "What hanging tree? I never heard that one."

"Tell her, Jo."

"It wasn't anything. Just an oak tree in the woods behind the old Burgess house."

"Where *Michael* lives. Ooohh . . . he has dreamy eyes."

"Jeez, Wendy! Stop drooling and let her finish."

Jo cleared her throat. "One day I was climbing the tree —"

"With Michael? Oh! I'd give anything —"

"Shut up!" Sharon hurled a pillow, hitting Wendy

smack in the head. "This happened before Michael, stupid. Go on, Jo."

"I found strands of rope. And marks, where the rope had cut into the tree. It was from a long time ago, when Emily Burgess hung herself." She bit into a chip with a satisfying crunch. Crisps, Michael called them. It was a much better name.

"*Jo*, go on!"

"Emily was heartbroken because the man she loved left her for somebody else. For her best friend."

"Well? Then what?" The girls leaned in closer.

"Emily's friend went crazy with grief. So crazy she lost her mind. And now she roams the woods behind her house looking for it."

No one spoke.

"And you know what? Emily's ghost is still out there."

A gust of wind brushed a flurry of leaves against the window and made the girls jump. "Can you hear her?" Jo whispered.

They listened. Rain splattered. The wind wailed.

"Emily's friend keeps roaming, trying to find that ghost so she can beg forgiveness. And get her mind back." Jo reached for a handful of Crackerjacks, congratulating herself on the story. Thanks to the mysterious note in Emily's unopened Christmas card, it was a much better story than the one she'd told Sharon two years ago. And it sounded completely believable.

Sharon shivered. "That story gives me the creeps. Who wants a float, to change the subject?"

They put spoonfuls of vanilla ice cream into tall,

fancy glasses, then poured in cream soda. Jo stirred her fizzy pink float and laughed. "It tickles my nose!"

"It tickles my throat," Marilyn giggled. "And my stomach. And my toes."

"You're crazy!" Sharon tossed another pillow. "OK, Jo. Now you have to tell us about Mack and the Elvis concert."

Jo repeated what Mack had told her, right down to Elvis's dazzling gold lamé suit with jeweled lapels, worth four thousand dollars. "Mack didn't get to meet him though, because right after the concert, he had to catch the train for Ottawa."

"Mack was going to *meet* him?" Sharon squealed.

"Of course. He always invites the most beautiful blonde to come backstage. And you know Mack." At least the beautiful blonde part was true. "He told her he was sorry he had to dash off."

"Wow!" The girls were impressed.

After the floats, they danced to records and sang along. Jo pretended to know the words. When it was her turn to dance without a partner she got so carried away she swiveled her hips right into the record player and sent the needle screeching across the record.

"Put on another one," said Sharon.

"Ooohhh . . ." Wendy sighed as the strains of "Love Me Tender" filled the room. "I want to save that for Michael. Don't you love the way he talks? Don't you think he's cute?"

"*Michael?*" Sharon shrieked. "His ears stick out and he's covered with freckles!"

"And he's so skinny!"

"So what?" Wendy leapt to Michael's defense. "He's a good basketball player. And a *great* shot. I saw him target-shooting in his back yard. Bull's eye every time."

"Did he let you try?"

"What was the gun like?"

"I don't know, just a gun."

Jo yanked the needle, putting an end to "Love Me Tender." Why didn't they shut up about Michael?

"You've seen his gun, haven't you, Jo?"

"Does he let you shoot it?"

Jo pretended not to hear. She put on a new record and turned the volume to full blast.

"Not so loud! My parents'll kill me!" Sharon knocked over Mack's records in her rush to turn down the volume. "Come on, Jo. Dance with me."

At lights-out time, Sharon supervised the arrangement of the sleeping bags so they fanned out like the spokes of a wheel. "Heads in the center so we can see with one flashlight," she said.

Snuggled inside their sleeping bags, the girls pored over Elvis, raving about his smouldering eyes and full lips.

Wendy sighed. "Michael's got lips like that."

Everyone but Jo laughed. "Come off it!"

"It's true. Look at his lips sometime, *just* his lips, not the rest of his face, and you'll see what I mean. They're *kissing* lips. I hope I'm the one he has to shark. Maybe he'll have to kiss the person, instead of just taking something."

"Yuck! Who would want to kiss Michael?"

"I would," said Wendy.

"Me too," said Diane.

Marilyn smirked. "Jo probably has, haven't you?"

"We know you were together all summer," Sharon sang, "building private little forts in the woods. For you know what . . ."

Jo buried her face in the warm flannel of her sleeping bag.

"Well?" Marilyn persisted. "Have you kissed Michael? Everybody says you did."

Jo poked out her head. "Who's everybody?"

"The whole class. So admit it. If you want to join the Presley Club, you have to tell a secret."

"If the whole class knows, it's hardly a secret."

"Yeah, Jo, but we want to hear it from you. What was it like? Did he, um . . ."

"French kissing is what she means," Diane said knowingly. "Did he do that, Jo?"

"Maybe they did more than that," Marilyn giggled. "Maybe they — you know." The girls were pink with anticipation.

"Come on, Jo," said Sharon. "I invited you to my party."

"You guys are nuts!" Wendy exclaimed. "Jo never did anything. How could she? She doesn't even know how it's done. Do you?"

Jo flushed with embarrassment.

"I knew it!" Wendy crowed. "Oh well. Maybe in a few years."

"Yeah, like twenty," said Marilyn. "We keep forgetting, she still has a babysitter."

"I do not."

"Don't lie, Jo. We know Mack goes to your place every Friday."

"She used to come and visit, that's all. Like friends do, you know?"

"*Friends?* Mack's seventeen! Why would she be friends with a baby like you?"

Jo searched for a Michael word, some brilliant *ipso facto* comeback. But her mind was blank.

"Ah, Joey! Don't look so sad," Sharon said. "We're just kidding. Where's *True Confessions*?" She snatched the magazine from Wendy's hand and flipped to a story about romance in the Rockies. "We'll take turns reading. Everybody gets one paragraph, then passes it on. I'll start." She read her paragraph in a low, whispery voice, while the others giggled over every second word.

When the story was finished, they lay in the dark playing a true confessions game. Jo made the appropriate responses and laughed with the others, but the whole time she felt it was an act.

What am I doing here? she wondered. The only reason they invited me was to get hold of Mack's records. And to find out more about Michael.

13

True confessions?

Jo had a few. She counted them silently, while the girls whispered their way through another sultry romance.

One. The person giggling in the sleeping bag wasn't really her.

Two. She didn't fit in.

Three. She didn't care.

Four. She wished she'd stayed home.

Five. She would've been happier reading a book or playing the piano. She could've tried some new duets with Mom. She could've worked on her story about the ghost of Emily Burgess. She could've phoned Michael again, before he left for the hockey game, and asked him what he thought about the Sputnik launching.

The world's first man-made satellite orbiting the earth! Michael would get some good words out of it. She pictured him on Monday, engaging Mr. West in a battle of words. Take *that*, interplanetary! Let's hear it for orbicular! And it's satellite in the lead!

But no use bringing up Sputnik. Sharon and the others would think it was a brand of mouthwash. And orbit? If "Orbit the Earth" was a new hit single by you-know-who they might be interested. Otherwise, forget it.

Next morning, before the others were awake, Jo gathered her things and tiptoed upstairs. Sharon's mother caught her as she crept past the kitchen. "You're not staying for breakfast?"

"No, thanks," Jo said. "I have to get home."

That evening, right after the supper dishes, Jo hurried up to Michael's. He had phoned earlier and invited her to the fort for a celebration. That's all he was saying.

Sharon had phoned, too. She hoped Jo wasn't mad about the teasing. Would she like to come to a pajama party next month and bring Mack's records? Jo said she was busy.

She left the well-lit street and plunged into the darkness of Michael's back yard. A faint light flickered through the trees and led her to the fort.

"Happy Sputnik!" Michael's face glowed in the lamplight.

"I knew it!" Jo looked around. "You've set things up again. I would've helped."

"Didn't take long," he said. "Soon as it stopped raining I hauled everything back out of the basement."

Jo smiled, pleased with how cozy the fort looked. A cable drum for a table. A crocheted tablecloth, ink-stained and torn in three places, but still lacy enough to be elegant. A tarp on the ground to keep out the fall dampness. One of Jo's grandma's old hooked rugs. And the *pièce de résistance* — as Mack would say — the coal-oil lamp Jo had scrounged from Grandad's shed.

To mark the occasion, Michael had made a choco-late cake with green peppermint icing. It was decorated with silver balls spelling the word *Sputnik*. "The shape is orbicular," he explained. "From the Latin *orbis* mean-ing circle."

"I brought some sparklers," Jo said. "The shape is a line, from the Latin . . . Oh, who cares. Once they're lit, they shoot out all over the place."

They wrapped themselves in blankets to keep warm, and after lighting the sparklers, ate the cake by lamplight. Then they blew out the flame and stared at the sky, hoping for a glimpse of the Russian-made satellite, twenty-two inches in diameter but bright as a second magnitude star. "Sputnik means traveling companion," Michael said. "Did you know that? It's orbiting the earth once every hour and thirty-five minutes. At eighteen thousand miles an hour."

"Mr. West will be sorry he lost the bet," said Jo. The previous week Mr. West had sworn the United States would launch the first man-made satellite, but Michael had bet it would be the Soviet Union.

"I'll take him a piece of cake as a consolation prize," Michael said.

Jo squinted at the sky. "Can you see it? I can't see anything but stars."

"We'd probably have a better chance of seeing it just before dawn," Michael said. "If the sky's clear."

"But even if we don't see it, we know it's there. Imagine! A silver ball, sending signals back to earth!" Jo felt a delicious shiver. It was such a big world out there.

"They'll put a person up next," said Michael.

Jo lay on her back, gazing at the sky. Anything was possible! It was a much bigger world than pajama parties or true confessions.

But confession pressed on her mind.

Mack's records were smeared with sticky finger-prints. Three were scratched. The one Sharon had stepped on was broken. *True Confessions* was torn, and two *Photoplay* magazines were crumpled and stained with cream soda.

Jo tried to convince herself the damage wasn't really so bad. But it was.

She decided to leave it for a while, hoping that something would happen.

But two weeks later she was still alive, Mack was still next door, and the wonder of Sputnik had not stopped the earth from turning. She couldn't put it off any longer. What was she, a fair-weather friend? No. She had to face the music.

After breakfast, she gathered up the magazines and

records and set off next door. The music from "The Volga Boat Song" droned in her mind, one tragic minor chord after another. She vowed she'd never play it again.

She trudged up the steps. What was the music this time, the "Funeral March of a Marionette?" No, more like the theme from "Dragnet."

Dum . . . da dum-dum . . . She knocked on the door, feeling pale and shaky. Her stomach spun like a turntable. Please let Mrs. Lamont answer, she prayed. I'll leave everything with her, I won't go inside . . .

Mack answered the door. "Jo! Come on in! You're just the person I want to see." She steered Jo into her room in spite of Jo's protests. "Have a seat. I've got something to tell you, something important. But first things first. Want some tea? Pop? How was the pajama party?"

"N-no, thanks," Jo stammered. "OK. The party, I mean. I mean —" She cleared her throat, took a deep breath and tried again. "It — it wasn't OK. I wrote down the names of the records and I'll buy you new ones as soon as I've saved up enough money. And I've taped the rip in the magazine, see? You can hardly notice. I'm sorry. I promised I'd be careful and I wasn't. At first I didn't let anybody touch them, but after — I forgot."

Mack sat down with the broken record and fit the two pieces together. "I trusted you. You know that, don't you? Breaking a trust is worse than breaking a record."

Jo felt a sudden surge of anger. Who was Mack, to talk about breaking a trust? All those Friday nights . . .

"Sometimes that trust can never be repaired.

Sometimes what's gone is gone for good. I'd hate for that to happen, Jo. You're as close to me as a little sister."

Little sister? Jo swallowed the hurt and forced out the words, "I thought I was a friend."

"You are!" Mack exclaimed. "Oh, Jo! I didn't mean — Don't go, please. I have to tell you something."

"Sure, Mack." Jo was too upset to listen. She brushed past Mack and headed for the door.

As soon as she got home, Jo attacked the piano. Minor scales, to match her mood. Four octaves, ascending and descending, with the loud pedal pressed to the floor.

She had almost finished the tricky A flat minor when it hit her. The trust Mack was talking about had nothing to do with broken records. It had everything to do with voices in the night.

That was the "something important" Mack wanted to tell her. Mack clearly wanted to explain and apologize.

Jo was still thinking about this after school the next day when she found the folded paper in her coat. She opened it eagerly, thinking it was an "I'm sorry" note Mack had slipped inside her pocket. But it wasn't. It was a drawing of a shark.

Jo gasped. It couldn't be. Michael wouldn't let it.

She glanced around the cloakroom to see if anyone had noticed. No one seemed to. The boys were all gone, and the few girls who remained were talking about homework. She scrunched up the paper and put it back in her pocket. It had to be meant for someone else.

"It's a mistake, isn't it?" she asked when she phoned Michael that evening. "They got the wrong coat."

There was a long pause. Then, "It's not the wrong coat."

"So it's me."

Michael said nothing.

"Who did the drawing? It's a bad one, so I know it wasn't you."

"I don't know."

"Oh, sure. I bet you know when it's going to happen, too."

Silence.

"Tell me!"

"I can't. I'm sorry."

Jo slammed down the receiver.

Each day became a torture of waiting.

Would it happen in the morning? Not if she left late. After school? Not if the boys were at basketball practice. Not if she hurried. And to be on the safe side, she took the long way home so she wouldn't be caught in the woods. She convinced herself that if she were prepared, it wouldn't happen. Because the rules said she had to be taken by surprise.

Then her school, like every other school in Victoria, was hit by a flu epidemic. For several days, most of the boys were away. Jo could let down her guard, at least for a while. She even escaped the flu.

It was on a Friday afternoon, the first of November, when she expected nothing more than to come home, grab a cupcake and practice the piano, that she heard her mother say, "Sit down, honey. I want to talk to you."

Something in her voice gave Jo a chill. "Is it Grandma? Grandad?"

"No, dear." Mom poured her a cup of tea. "It's Mack."

Jo lowered the cup with shaking fingers. "Mack's . . . dead?"

"No, dear. Mack's in trouble."

14

Fudge, fudge
Tell the judge
Mommy's having a baby
It ain't no girl
It ain't no boy
It's just a newborn baby
Wrap it up in tissue paper
Throw it down the elevator —

Jo woke up sweating, the chant clear in her mind. It was a springtime chant, words strung together, with a group of girls and a skipping rope slapping the pavement, a chant sung with daffodils in the background. The words never meant anything. Until now.

Mack was in trouble. Mack was having a baby.

"But she's not married," Jo had said when her mother told her. Hoping, stupidly, that somehow that would make it impossible.

"No, she's not," Mom said. "Her whole life ahead of her, and now this. She'll have to quit school, won't be able to graduate —"

"But she's going to be a teacher."

"Not now she isn't. One mistake, and her whole life is thrown away."

Throw it down the elevator. Is that what you did with mistakes? *Wrap it up in tissue paper . . .*

Jo remembered when Mrs. Hicks up the street lost her baby. What was it, a miscarriage? Maybe that would happen to Mack?

Mom didn't think so. "It's possible, but not likely. What baffles me is how this could have happened. She was never allowed to date, never had a boyfriend. Her father kept such a tight rein on her. He'll kill her when he finds out."

Jo could hardly breathe. "He doesn't know?"

Mom shook her head. "Mrs. Lamont told me this morning. She wants it kept quiet. I'm only telling you because you've always been so close to Mack. I'm surprised she didn't tell you herself. She's known for a couple of weeks."

So that was what Mack had wanted to tell her the day Jo took back the records. "What will she do?"

"She'll have a baby," Mom had said. "What else? There are no other choices."

It ain't no girl, it ain't no boy . . . But it would be. One or the other. And it would be beautiful, Mack's baby. And Jo would babysit. She'd take along a bag of tricks like Mack used to do. Make Baked Alaska, read stories, have Choose Days . . . She smiled, pleased with the thought. Until she realized — it wouldn't be like that.

Before going to bed, Jo had asked if they could give Mack a baby shower. She pictured their living room strung with paper chains, her and Ian's old wicker bassinet decorated and filled with presents. Maybe she could make a wreath with rattles and diaper pins and pacifiers. If she started now, she could embroider a bib. She'd seen them in the Metropolitan Five and Dime — little bibs with pictures that you filled in with colored thread. "And I could make sandwiches. You know the roll-up kind with cream cheese and asparagus? Could I, Mom?"

"Jo," Mom said, "I don't think you understand. Mack's got herself in trouble and made a mess of things. It's not something she or anybody else wants to celebrate. Her mother's sick about it. It's the worst thing that could have happened."

"But it's Mack! How can you say she's made a mess of things?"

"Think, Jo!" Mom said angrily. "What position is she in to have a baby? She's only seventeen, still in high school. At Christmas she's going to Toronto. She'll have the baby there." She gave an exasperated sigh. "All that promise thrown away."

"But she could get married, couldn't she? And stay here?"

"She refuses to get married, which makes the whole

business even worse. She won't say who the father is, only that he's in grade twelve. And of course he won't have to quit school. Not like her. When in heaven's name did it happen? And where? At least it wasn't here. We always trusted Mack. She never had boys over."

It wasn't a question. But Jo had looked her mother straight in the eye and said, "Never."

Fudge, fudge, tell the judge . . .

She sat up in bed, pulled back the curtains and stared out the window. If she could see the satellite, everything would be fine. But she couldn't. There was no brightness in the sky, not a single star.

Tell the judge . . .

She wouldn't tell. Even though she knew who and when and where. It'd happened in her house, in her own living room, on a Friday night when she and Ian were asleep. Alan had phoned to make sure Jo's parents were out, then come to the door and tapped the signal so Mack would let him in. Sure, Mack liked staying to watch the Gillespies' "better" TV. Sure, Alan was working. And got off just in time to stop by on his way home.

All those times at Willows Beach meeting Alan — it was never a coincidence. Mack had planned it ahead of time, then invited Jo. "But I promised. I have to go." Is that what she told her dad?

And all those other times, when Jo was younger — at the Crystal Gardens Pool, the library — Jo was the excuse, the chance for Mack to break away. Her dad probably thought, what could happen with a little kid tagging along?

And afterwards, Mack had given Jo presents.

First thing next morning, Jo filled a paper bag, ran over to Mack's and burst into her room. She dumped the bag's contents on the bed and yelled, "Here! You can have it all back!"

Mack opened her mouth in surprise as pop-it beads fell over the edge of her bed and rolled across the floor. Earrings, brooches and necklaces glinted on the bedspread. "Jo! What —"

"You *used* me! All those times you took me places — you told your dad you had to babysit, didn't you? *Didn't* you? I was just an excuse!"

"Calm down! That's not true."

"You could've just *asked* me not to tell. I kept your secrets. You didn't have to pay me off!"

"I gave you things because I wanted to."

"When Alan came sneaking over I wouldn't have told. Ian might've. But not me! I wish I had! It wouldn't have happened then, would it? You wouldn't have gotten into trouble and you wouldn't have to go away!"

"Jo, listen —"

"I should've told. It's all my fault." Angrily, she fought back the tears. This wasn't supposed to happen. She wanted to scream at Mack, not break down and cry. She wanted to hate her.

"*Your* fault? Take the world on your shoulders, why don't you? How could it possibly be your fault? Anyway —" She patted her stomach. "It wouldn't have mattered if you'd told. The baby's due the middle of May. So figure it out."

Jo counted back nine months and landed in mid-August. At Willows Beach. Around the time she left

Mack and Alan and took the bus home by herself. That was supposed to make her feel better?

Mack put her hand under Jo's chin and forced her to look up. "Listen. Life's a bag of Choose Days. Crumpled-up bits of paper, remember? You reach in and take your pick. The only difference is, most of the time you can see what's written. And if you have half a brain you know what you're getting into. I made the wrong choice." She attempted to laugh. "Me, Mack the Invincible! I never dreamed it would happen to me."

"You weren't even married!"

Mack sighed. "It's all so black and white with you, isn't it? One day you'll see that life isn't that simple."

Jo gave a loud sniff. "Why don't you just marry him?"

"I don't want to. My mother says our sole purpose for being on this earth is to get married and have children. It's our duty, she says. That's all there is, she says. Well, I don't believe it. I'm still going to college and I'm going to have a wonderful life."

Jo picked up a silver chain and worked at the knots. "Aren't you forgetting something?" she said bitterly. "What about your baby?"

Mack moved to the dressing table, untied her ponytail and began brushing her hair. "Mom and I are going to Toronto to spend Christmas with my aunt. Then I'm going to a Home for Unwed Mothers." Ten strokes, fifteen . . . For a long time, the only sound was the sweep of the brush and the crackle of static. "I'll have the baby there and give it up for adoption."

Give up sounded like failure. What you say when

you can't guess a riddle. *Give it up.* Like throw it up. No, throw it down. *Throw it down the elevator . . .*

"How can you?" Jo blurted out angrily. "It's a *baby* you're talking about, not some old piece of jewelry. All you ever do is give stuff away. When you're tired of it. Or when you think you can get something out of it. How can you do that with a baby?"

Twenty strokes, twenty-five . . . Mack put down the brush and faced Jo through the mirror. "Whatever you think — don't think it's easy. It breaks my heart, the thought of giving up this baby. And it won't get any easier. I'll always wonder, probably forever — what if?

"But I have to think, what would be best for the baby? Sure, I'd love to have a baby of my own. But I'm not ready. And babies grow up. I can't support a child, neither can Alan. And if we end up feeling trapped and start hating each other because we had to get married, what then? Believe me, I've thought about this long and hard. More than anything, I want this baby to have a good home. I want him — or her — to be wanted. And treasured.

"So how can I give it up? I can because of you. And Ian. I see how happy you are with your family, and how much your parents love you. If it hadn't been for someone like me, someone who gave her baby up for adoption, none of that would've happened." Mack's eyes welled up with tears. "There's a saying that the greatest act of love is letting go. I think — Hey, are you all right?"

Jo was no longer listening. She felt a terrible numbness, as if Mack had pulled a magic wand out of her bag of tricks and turned her into stone.

15

"Jo! I thought you knew. I thought — Wait! Don't go like this!"

Out the door, down the steps, onto the street, up the hill. *If it hadn't been for someone like me . . .*

Mack's words tumbled inside Jo's head, becoming as tangled as the bits and pieces of jewelry. *Giving up, letting go, someone like me . . .* She thought she heard Mack calling her name. She thought she heard her mother.

But it wasn't her real mother. Her mother was someone like Mack, someone who'd had a baby and given her up.

She thought she heard Michael yelling from his upstairs window, "Hey Jo, wait!"

Knock knock.
Who's there?
Jo.
Jo who?
She didn't know.

She wasn't even Jo anymore. Someone had made a mess of things. She was that someone's mistake.

She walked into the woods at the top of the hill and sank down against an oak tree. The ground felt damp. A gusty November wind scattered leaves. Bare branches waved like the arms of ghosts.

Everything she had told Ian was true. Mom and Dad weren't his real parents. Jo wasn't his sister.

Everything she had told herself was a lie. Family story? She didn't have one.

She stared off into space as if a part of her was missing and she was waiting for it to come home. But where was home?

The sky was gray and miserable, heavy with rain. The air felt clammy and cold.

Jo didn't feel the cold. All she felt was empty.

The kitchen smelled of lunch — minestrone soup and freshly-baked bread. Jo would have none of it. She stormed into the dining room, gripped the back of a chair to keep her hands from trembling, and shouted, "Why didn't you tell me?"

"Tell you what?" Dad put down his spoon and gave her a worried look.

"You know what!" Jo cried. "My whole life! My whole life I thought you were my parents and you're not. And I had to hear it from Mack."

"Oh, boy," Dad whispered under his breath. "Jo, honey . . . sit down, we'll explain."

"*Explain?* It's a bit late for that, isn't it? Try eleven years too late."

"We meant to tell you, of course we did. We decided to wait till you were older."

"How old? *Forty?*"

"We were afraid if we told you too soon, you wouldn't understand," Mom said. "The last thing we wanted was for you to be hurt."

"Hurt? You have no idea. Everything I thought I knew — everything —" Jo's stomach reeled and her voice shook with despair. "I used to know who I was. Now I'm a no one. I'm just a nothing that somebody got rid of."

"Oh, honey." Mom reached out her arms to comfort her.

Jo pushed her away and stumbled from the room.

If she could sleep and wake up it would all be a dream.

But Jo couldn't sleep.

Flicka whimpered outside her room. Mom, Dad and Ian took turns knocking on her door. Did she want something to eat? Could they talk? Please, Jo —

If she could sleep and wake up it would all be a story. An idea gone wild. Out of control.

But no sleep, no dream, no story could repair the damage. Without warning, everything she thought she knew was swept away. Everything. As if it had been struck by an avalanche.

Whooosh! There goes what you thought was your life.

And an avalanche did more than sweep away. It buried things, like the truth about her birth. Who was she? Where was she from?

Her parents had kept those things hidden.

Lying on her bed, curled up in a ball, Jo hugged herself tightly to hold back the anger. To keep it from bursting out and breaking her into a million nameless pieces.

16

It was late afternoon when Jo consented to come out of her room. She only did it because anger gave her the energy. And because she figured she might as well hear what they had to say. Then it would be done. Over with. Terminated.

Her family — that was a laugh — had already gathered in the living room. Jo slumped into a corner of the couch.

Mom started the little talk. "Do you remember when Mrs. Hicks lost her baby?"

Ian looked puzzled. "Yeah."

"That happened to me. Many times."

Jo felt Mom's eyes on her, but refused to look her way. Instead, she stared into the fireplace. It was unusual for Dad to light a fire in the afternoon, even a cold and gloomy afternoon like this one. A sure sign they wanted this moment to be special. Well, too bad. They had drawn Jo out of her bedroom but nothing they said would make any difference.

She concentrated on the flames. Red, orange, yellow. Bits of bluish-purple . . .

"We wanted a baby so badly," Dad said. "And when we learned your mother couldn't have her own, we decided to adopt one."

"We waited a long time," Mom said. "Then one day the adoption agency told us about a woman who had a baby. A beautiful baby girl that she wasn't able to keep."

"That was Jo?"

"Yes, Ian. Joanne Catherine."

"Is that how you got me, too?" Ian asked.

"Yes, honey." Mom ruffled his hair. "And we love you every bit as much as if you were our own."

"Didn't she love me? The lady that had me?"

"Oh, yes. We never met her, of course, but we know she loved you very much. She just couldn't be a parent. And she wanted you to have parents who could look after you, and love you as much as she did."

"Oh." He paused. "And Jo's other mom was like that, too?"

"Yes, dear."

"Will she — that lady — will she come and take me away?" Ian sounded worried.

"No, dear. She doesn't know who we are and she doesn't know where you are. But she'd be very proud of you. And the woman who had Jo would be very proud of her."

"We're sorry we didn't tell you before. And for Jo to find out from Mack —" Dad reached out to pat Jo's hand but she snatched it away. "Of course it was a shock."

"Nobody knew," Mom said. "None of the neighbors. They didn't. Only Mrs. Lamont, and I only told her because I thought it would help, because of Mack's situation. Jo, please understand that." Her voice was pleading. "It's not like everyone knew except you. We realize how wrong it was not to tell you from the beginning. We wanted to wait until you were older, but you grew up so fast . . ."

"That's OK," said Ian. "So you didn't find me in a basket on the porch?"

Mom laughed. "Of course not! We brought you home from the hospital, like all newborn babies."

"And Jo didn't drop me on my head?"

"She was too little to carry you," Dad said. "But sometimes she sat right there on that couch and held you. Very carefully."

Ian smiled. "Can I tell Wayne?"

"If you like. It's no secret."

"Can I go now?"

"Yes, dear. Of course."

"I'm going, too," said Jo.

"Wait, Jo. Your mother and —"

"She's not my mother." Quickly, she left the room.

Rain streamed down the window.

No secret, Dad had said.

Everybody knew. Jo was sure of it. Her grand-parents, all the relatives, even her obnoxious cousin, Ron, probably knew.

She remembered the family reunion the previous spring, when everyone had gathered to celebrate Grandma's birthday. She and Ian had made a picture of Grandma as a young girl in Sweden, hair flying out in braids, arms outstretched as if she were embracing the world. Ian had drawn an enormous sun, and they took turns coloring the rays in canary yellow and vermilion red. They colored the sides of the picture black, since it was midnight. Then, to make it really dazzling, they stuck on gold stars and wrote in silver crayon across the top, *Dancing in the Midnight Sun*.

Grandma loved it. Cousin Ron didn't, though. "Why the black sky and stars? When there's a mid-night sun there's no night!" He cackled loudly. "You've missed the whole point!"

Jo had glared at her oldest cousin. "The point is, the midnight sun is special. There might be darkness all around, but whenever the midnight sun shines, you celebrate."

Celebrate what? She stared at the wet, gray world outside her window. Where was the midnight sun, now? Where was the sun, period? Talk about missing the point.

Then there was Aunt Lizzie's comment. After admiring the midnight sun picture, she had waltzed over to Jo and gushed, "What a talented pair you are, you and Ian! Your parents are so *lucky* the way you turned out."

Turned out? She made it sound like they were a *Chatelaine* Meal of the Month.

Were the relatives surprised, then? Had they been holding their collective breath, waiting to see if the adopted kids turned into monsters?

And Grandma's comments about Jo's nose. Whenever Jo walked into her grandparents' house she smelled something delicious — gingersnaps, Swedish meatballs flavored with allspice, roasted lamb with dill sauce, sour cherry fruit soup . . . It was a ritual — stop and sniff, guess what was cooking, walk into the kitchen and say, "My nose was right."

Grandma would always laugh. "You must have the Anderson nose."

Lies, lies. Her nose came from somebody else.

All those times she had pored over the family albums at Grandma's, studying pictures of Mom as a little girl. She had searched for resemblances and found them — in the slight figure, the heart-shaped face, the hair that refused to curl. What about that? Lies.

And at home, the albums from Dad's side of the family, showing him with the smile that matched hers. Ha! All lies.

No one ever said she was wrong. No one ever said she was only seeing what she wanted to see.

And the way her relatives praised her piano playing? And said she got that talent from her mother? More lies. But they let her grow up believing them.

The one thing that confused everyone was her

story-writing. Where does she get that from? they wondered. Now she knew.

She remembered her thoughts the night of the Sputnik celebration. *It was such a big world out there . . .*

Somewhere in that world she had a whole other family — mother, father, grandparents, aunts and uncles, maybe brothers and sisters. People she couldn't see or hear or touch, but who were there all the same.

Somewhere out there was her real mother, the woman who had given her up. How old was she? Did she look like Jo? Did she have brown hair, hazel eyes, a ski-jump nose and a tiny mole under her left eye? Did she play the piano and make up stories? Was she happy? Did she have a wonderful life? Did she ever think of the baby she gave away?

Jo stared out at the rain. As far as her life was concerned, Grandad Anderson might as well have died in the avalanche. That night in the mountains, the angel might as well have whispered in someone else's ear.

17

For the first two weeks of November, there was no sky. Only clouds — steel-gray, slate-gray, leaden-gray — oppressively heavy, like elephants lumbering above the earth. Rain fell for days upon days until Jo thought she'd drown in the relentless dripping, pattering, pounding of it.

Then came a wind that slashed raw, bitter cold through layers of clothing right through to the bone.

In spite of the wind and rain Jo refused her dad's offers of a ride and continued to bike to school. Once inside, she removed her rubber boots, hung up her rain-coat to dry in the steaming reek of the cloakroom, then went to her desk. Because of the weather, her mother packed her a lunch. Thank heavens. She wouldn't have to listen to Mom pretending that everything was normal, at least not at lunch time.

She began staying late after school. There was always something to do — wash the blackboards, pin drawings up on the walls. When Mr. West ran out of jobs, she marked papers for the primary teachers.

She went back to taking the shortcut through the woods, certain that the sharking wouldn't happen in the rain. The boys might be morons but they weren't completely stupid. And besides — what was she afraid of? She'd lost her self. Nothing anyone could take would hurt as much as that. Nothing. Not ever.

On a Monday night, the third week of November, Jo looked out her window and saw a slice of moon, clear and cold and white. She heard the swish of the occasional car passing through the neighborhood, but other than that, silence. No wind. No rain. Tomorrow there could be sunshine.

Later that night, she dreamed of the sun. She saw it clearly — a ray of sunlight that broke through the mist at Willows Beach.

The beach was deserted. A small boat drifted in the bay. Three people were in it, a man, woman and boy. Something about the way the boy stood reminded her of Ian, but as Jo strained for a closer look, the mist rolled in and the boat disappeared.

She wished she'd brought her shoes. The sand felt damp and cold on her bare feet. But it was deliciously empty. Not one footprint marked it, apart from her own. She could write her life on this sand and only the sea would read it, when the tide came in to wash her words away.

She was surprised to see two young women walking towards her, one dressed in black, the other in white. Like piano keys. They moved as if in a wedding procession. She could almost hear the organ above the slapping sea and squawking gulls.

The woman in white held out a shell. A pink shell that reminded Jo of Mack's painted toenails. Taking it from the woman's outstretched hand, she opened it and found a baby girl inside. Tiny and perfect, curled up in the rosy iridescence of the seashell. Jo asked, "What should I do with her?"

The woman in black chanted, "Wrap it up in tissue paper!" But the woman in white smiled a scimitar smile and said, "Every day's a Choose Day." Then they vanished, leaving no footprints.

Jo closed the shell carefully. She was about to put it in her pocket when a gull swooped down, snatched it from her hand and flew out to sea.

"Bring me back!" Jo shouted. She ran after the gull, sinking deeper and deeper, until the water drowned her cries.

Jo woke abruptly. Her comforter was bunched around her head and shoulders. Her feet were freezing. She rearranged the covers and remembered the dream. Every detail was clear, except for the faces of the women.

She fell back into an uneasy sleep, disturbed by the reappearance of the women and something else — a sinister image that circled the bay and the edges of her dream. It wasn't until she was getting dressed the next morning that she recognized the image as that of a shark.

A sign. Today was the day. Unless it was raining . . .

She pulled back the curtains. A dusting of frost lay like gauze over the yard. And in the sky, nothing but blue.

So. Today was the day.

Jo got up and dressed. Her fingers fumbled with the buttons on her blouse. She was almost finished when she noticed the brooch pinned to the collar. The scimitar brooch, left on the blouse and forgotten. The one piece of jewelry she hadn't thrown back at Mack.

She was already outside and waiting when Michael came coasting down the hill. Before he could stop, she kicked off and pedaled beside him. "Know what, Michael? I know it's today. And I don't care. You can do your stupid sharking whenever or wherever you like."

Michael gave her a what-are-you-talking-about look.

"Oh, yeah. Mr. Innocent. Your friends are probably waiting in the woods. Hey! Maybe they've even got your precious gun. But so what? I don't care. I'm taking the shortcut, same as usual. And know what else? I might decide to shark you instead. So watch it, Featherstone."

"What's gotten into you? You never talked like that before."

"Well maybe I'm not the same, all right? So you can like it or lump it." She swerved to avoid a frost-licked puddle and almost skidded in the mud.

She arrived at the bike racks half-relieved, half-disappointed the boys hadn't got her on the way to school. Maybe lunchtime?

Nothing happened.

After school she asked Mr. West if she could help in the classroom.

"Again?" he said. "My goodness, you've turned over a new leaf. What's happening? You were always the first one out the door."

"I felt like a change." She leaned out the window to shake the dusty chamois.

"How's your piano playing?" Mr. West asked. "Don't you usually practice after school?"

Jo carefully wrote the next day's date on the board. "Nope, that's another change. Now I practice after supper." The truth was, lately she'd hardly touched the piano.

"I liked the composition you wrote this morning, about the baby found in the seashell. Where on earth do you get your ideas?"

Jo shrugged. "Can I do the window display?"

"Certainly!" Mr. West tucked a stack of arithmetic books under his arm and picked up his empty coffee cup. "I'll be in the staff room if you need me."

A few moments later, Michael appeared. "Do you want to bike home with me?"

"I said I'd help Mr. West."

"Why are you such a teacher's pet all of a sudden?"

"I'm not!" She turned her back and began changing the window display. Down came the Remembrance Day poppies, up went the cut-paper snowflakes. In a few months it would be hearts, followed by kites and daffodils. It was comforting to know there were still some things she could count on.

"Come up to the fort, then. It'll be cold but at least it's stopped raining."

She looked over her shoulder, surprised that Michael was still there. "Don't you have basketball?"

"Practice ends at three-thirty. It's twenty to four."

"Aren't you going to Donny's?"

"Not today."

"Oh. Well, I want to finish this."

"Come up later then. I'll be in the fort after supper."

Oh, sure. It was all part of the plan. Get Michael to find out when she was leaving, then lie in wait. Well, they could wait all they liked. Sharking didn't bother her anymore, not one bit. It was a joke. One huge monumental joke.

She finished taping the snowflakes to the window and dusted off the chalk ledge. Then she put on her coat and walked leisurely out of the classroom.

A basketball from the outside court thumped past her head as she came down the front steps of the school. She caught it on the rebound.

"Watch it!" she yelled to the boys on the court.

"Sor-ree," Bob laughed. "Toss it over."

"OK." She deliberately threw the ball in the opposite direction.

"Not smart, Gillespie," Donny shouted as Jo headed for the bike racks. "Your time's almost up."

"Yeah," she called over her shoulder. "Can't you see I'm petrified?"

"You should be!" Doug yelled.

She was halfway down the street when she heard the bikes speeding up behind her. Nothing to worry about. This wasn't sharking. Sharking was lying in ambush then pounce and grab, that's what Wendy said, that's what everybody said.

So why was she pedaling faster? And why should she believe Wendy? Or Sharon or Mack or anybody?

"Hey, Jo, wait up! What's your hurry? You're not scared, are you?"

She turned the corner, trying to outpace them, but in seconds the boys had caught up. Three bikes hemmed her in on either side. There was no way to go but down the street that led to the woods.

"Scared yet?" Gil grazed her front wheel so their pedals touched.

"No!" Jo spat the word in his face. At the same time she gave his shin a ferocious kick, making him cry out in surprise.

Was she scared?

No. Now that it was happening, she was terrified.

The rush of adrenaline made her pedal harder but the woods were closing in, dark in the late afternoon, and the boys were not falling behind. Please let a car come, she prayed. Then they'd have to split up, then she could break away.

But a car didn't come. The boys forced her across the street and into the woods, three in front and three behind, single file along the narrow path until they reached the pond.

She was forced to stop when they did. She couldn't

go through them or around them. No matter how hard she imagined otherwise, her bike was a bike, not a tempermental stallion only she could handle. It was not going to rear up and flash its hooves in their faces.

But she could. With a sudden, unexpected move she threw down her bike and struck out at the boys, hitting faces and chests and shoulders and arms, not caring that they did nothing but dodge her fists and laugh. And just when she thought she could make a run for it, a figure in a Frankenstein mask leapt out of the bushes by the pond, grabbed her coat and pushed her down in the mud.

"Go ahead and take it!" she screamed. "Take whatever you like! Seven against one? That's real brave, isn't it?" She tried to pull off the mask while the figure fumbled with the buttons on her coat. "I know it's you, Michael! I'll get you for this, just wait!"

The boys formed a circle, laughing. "Whatcha gonna take, huh?"

"Take her coat!"

"Nah, rip off a button!"

"Throw her shoes in the pond!"

They shouted one suggestion after another until someone noticed the brooch on her blouse. "Take that sword pin she's always bragging about!"

Michael's hand reached towards the brooch. His fingers clasped the sword.

At that moment, Jo thrust her head forward and bit into the back of his hand.

"Yeoww!" Michael hollered. But he wouldn't let go. Neither would Jo. Without loosening her grip, she yelled through clenched teeth, and although her words were barely recognizable, the anger behind them was clear. "No one's hurting me anymore! Not you, not Mack, not anybody!"

"All right, all right! Keep the flipping sword!" He let go.

Jo released her hold and stumbled to her feet. She spat out what she thought was the taste of blood. Her breath came in gasps. Her voice rose to a shriek. "You think — you think I want it? You think I care? Take it! Just take it!" She yanked the scimitar from its scabbard. The chain broke as she knew it would, but what did it matter? Every other connection was broken — Mack, her mother, now Michael — why not the chain? Viciously, she hurled it into Michael's face.

Michael flinched. No one spoke.

Jo stormed past the boys, her body flaring with rage. No one stopped her as she picked up her bike and sped off in the darkness.

18

Once, Jo could have talked to her parents. Now they were strangers.

She refused to talk to Mack. Whenever she phoned or came over, Jo made excuses.

As for Michael . . .

On Wednesday, the day after the sharking, nothing was said. Normally the boys would bring the ripped-off trophy and brag about it on the playground. But there was no sign of Jo's broken scimitar. For all she knew it was still in the woods, trampled in the mud. And good riddance.

Starting Wednesday morning, Jo left before Michael, and biked to school alone. She stopped helping her teacher and came straight home to the piano. Two weeks without playing had hurt her more than anyone else. The piano, the connection of hands to keyboard, the flow of music — that was a constant, something she could rely on.

With Flicka lying at her feet, she immersed herself in scales and chords, dominant sevenths, staccato sixths, four octaves of arpeggios rising and falling to the driving beat of the metronome. Faster, faster, *vivace, presto, spiritoso*.

The pieces she played — gavottes, preludes, sonatinas — were always *allegro*. Anything slow, anything quiet or tender — *adagio, pianissimo* — would make her cry.

Once, Jo used to end every practice session with show tunes from musicals. *Showboat* and *Oklahoma!* were Mom's favorites. She knew all the words and loved to sing along while working in the kitchen. Jo would sing, too. Not anymore.

Jo practiced until supper. Helped with the dishes, as usual. Then retreated to her room. After doing her homework, she wrote stories. Stories about who her real family might be. Family stories. Fairy tales.

At the end of November, Jo received a Christmas card in the mail. It was the card she'd found in Michael's cupboard. On the front, a host of heavenly angels. Inside, a note written in a flowing, ink-smudged hand. *Dearest Emily. Please let me explain. Your forgiveness means everything. Your loving friend, B.* Underneath, in Michael's backhanded script, was a P.S. *Me too.*

Tucked inside the card, wrapped in tissue paper, was a gold scimitar attached to a broken chain. "Thanks, Michael," Jo said bitterly. "Thanks for nothing."

He wanted to explain? Explain what? She'd been there, in case he'd forgotten. And forgiveness? Ha! Angrily, she flung the scimitar across her bedroom floor, then went to the piano to practice.

Minor scales, loud, hard and fast. That was the way to fix Michael. Pound him right out of existence.

"Easy on that pedal!" Dad called from the kitchen. "You'll wake the dead."

"Too bad," Jo mumbled.

Wake the dead. The phrase made her think of Emily Burgess, all those years ago. And the mysterious B.

She left the piano and sat down for supper, wondering if Emily ever forgave her friend. For some reason, Jo couldn't picture Emily as a fair-weather friend. She didn't want to see herself that way, either. But forgive Michael?

"Jo, take the plate, for goodness sake. My arm's breaking."

"All right, all right." She stifled a groan at what looked suspiciously like liver. "Is this . . ."

"*Chatelaine* Meal of the Month," Dad said. "Can't beat that."

"Oh, yes I can." She could beat liver and Gil and the whole lot of them, especially Michael and his pathetic attempt at begging forgiveness. She could beat her phony parents, too, and never forgive them for lying.

"Watch this." She buried a speck of liver in a forkful of whipped potatoes and washed the mouthful down with a glass of milk. "See? Didn't even taste it. I can beat anything and still come out smiling. See?" She pushed her face into a smile and helped herself to more potatoes, corn and onion rings.

"Know what happened to Mack if she didn't eat everything on her plate?" Ian said. "She got it again the next meal, and nothing else. So if she didn't eat her porridge for breakfast she got it for lunch, then supper, then breakfast the next day. You wouldn't do that to us, would you, Mom?"

"She's not your real mom," Jo muttered.

"What's that, dear?"

"I was just saying to Ian, why don't you ever stop talking about Mack? Like she's Queen of the Universe or something. She's just a stupid dumb teenager. And you're just a stupid dumb kid."

"What does that make you?" Ian shot back. "You're —"

"Cut it out, you two," Mom said. "Or you won't be coming to Grandma's with me tonight."

"I'm not anyway." Jo flattened her potatoes with the back of her fork. Lines, crossings. Criss-cross. "I'm going to Michael's." The words were out before she knew it. "We're working on a homework project. On sharks and barracudas. Man-eating fish that devour stupid dumb kids." She flashed her teeth.

"*Mom!*" Ian protested.

"I know, cut it out." Jo pushed back her chair. "Can I be excused? Please?"

"Make sure you're back by eight," Dad said. "Got that?"

"Yes, yes." She gathered up her books, put on her coat and slipped some matches into her pocket. And because it would be cold — freezing, probably — she took her sleeping bag. Maybe she'd stay out all night.

The sky glittered with stars. Like the night of the Sputnik celebration, Jo remembered. The last time she'd been in the fort.

Everything was set up. Heavy tarp on the ground, hooked rug to sit on, cable drum table. Lacy tablecloth, stiff with frost. And in the center, the oil lamp. Everything set up, as if Michael was expecting her.

Or maybe he was using the fort with his friends. Maybe this was their meeting place for target practice. For shooting his stupid gun.

Jo unrolled her sleeping bag and wrapped it snugly around her shoulders. What was she thinking? Homework on *sharks*? What an excuse.

The Christmas card baffled her. Why would Michael care? He had tons of friends. Everybody liked him. The life of the party, that was Michael. The creep.

Still . . . he must have picked up the little scimitar. Maybe even gone back for it, rescued it from the mud. He must have cleaned it and given it a polish. It was shining when Jo unwrapped it. So was the chain. Broken, but shining. She could probably fix it. But nothing could put it right.

She shivered, and remembered the matches. Michael's bedroom window overlooked the woods. As Jo lit the lamp, she caught herself hoping Michael would see the glow and come outside.

Why? a part of her cried out. Why, after what he did?

Jo whispered the answer, making clouds in the cold night air. "Because I miss him."

The lamplight wasn't much, but it gave the illusion of warmth. Before replacing the chimney, Jo took the shark drawing from her pocket and held it to the flame. "Good riddance," she said. The shark blackened and curled to ash.

"Good riddance to who?" Jo looked up. There was Michael, loaded down with blankets and a thermos. "If you mean me, you don't get any cocoa."

"No, I don't mean —" She broke off suddenly. "Yes! Yes, I do!" She leapt to her feet. "Good riddance to you! How *could* you? You — you *creep!*"

He poured a cup of cocoa and offered it to her.

"Forget it!" She knocked it from his hand. Hot liquid splashed over her pants. "Ow! Now look what you've done! That's it, I'm going."

"Well, good riddance to you too, then!" he shouted. "You think I wanted to do that sharking? You think it was such a lark? I'm sorry, I'm sorry, I'll say it a million times, all right? Oh, it's fine for you to be different. Everybody knows that and accepts it. Me? I'm still the weird kid from England who talks funny. Don't you get it? I want — Oh, you're too thick to understand. Well? What are you waiting for? Go! Go on! Go home!"

"I can't!" she blurted out. "I'm adopted!" The words surprised her. She hadn't meant to tell him.

"So — " He looked at her for a moment. "Oh."

Michael at a loss for words was the last thing Jo expected. She watched him pick up the cup she had knocked to the ground, carefully wipe it with the edge of a blanket, and refill it with cocoa. "Want some?"

Jo heaved a sigh and sat down. "Sure."

For a long time they sat without speaking, passing the cocoa back and forth. Curls of steam rose from the cup, carrying the fragrance of chocolate. A warm circle of light glowed between them.

"I found out from Mack," Jo said. "My parents never even told me. I hate them."

"Adopt is from the Latin *adoptare*, meaning to choose."

"Oh, Michael! Can't you shut up about your Latin, for once? We're talking about my life, not some stupid word."

"You were chosen. That's what I meant to say. That makes you extra special, don't you think?"

"Yeah, like I was chosen for the sharking. That makes me really special." She sniffed loudly, and took another sip of cocoa. "I want to belong, same as you. I thought I did. Now I don't know who I am anymore. It's like a part of me has gone away and . . . and left someone else in my place. Some crazy, certifiable person. When I was fighting and when I bit your hand — that wasn't me. Don't you ever feel like someone else is taking over?"

"Sometimes. That sharking thing wasn't me. But I wanted — you know."

"I used to make up stories about being adopted, and how my real parents were rich and famous and would one day come and take me away."

"Everybody does that," Michael said. "Thinks

they've got real parents, better parents, somewhere else. I do, when I'm mad at my mum and dad. It doesn't mean I'm certifiable. Neither are you."

"But my stories turned out to be true."

"Would you want your other parents to show up and take you away? You'd have to go to a different house, maybe a different town. And what if they had other kids? They might have rotten kids, not nice ones like Ian. I think you should stay where you are. You're lucky, actually. You know your parents really wanted you. And they're awfully nice."

Jo shrugged. Nice? Maybe. But her *real* parents would be nicer. Rich. Intelligent. Talented. And they would live in an exotic place like Hawaii or Australia. What's more, they would never lie to her or keep things hidden. They would be scrupulously honest.

"You didn't mean it back then, did you? How you couldn't go home because you were adopted?" Michael gestured to her sleeping bag. "Were you planning to camp out here?"

"Maybe next summer," Jo said. "When it's not so cold."

"Can you see the new Sputnik?"

Jo squinted her eyes. "No. I never saw the old one."

"It's still up there. And this new one's got a dog."

Come to think of it, Dad had mentioned the dog at supper the other night, and made a typically corny joke about calling the new satellite Muttnik. "What kind of dog?"

"A mongrel terrier, I think, but does it matter? She's Laika, the first dog in space."

Poor thing, Jo thought. All by herself in a satellite, orbiting the earth. Like me, orbiting what I thought was my family. Looking for a place to land.

19

Saturday, November 30th.

As soon as she got up, Jo put an X through the date and flipped her calendar to December. Only thirteen days until her birthday. And this year it would fall on a Friday.

It had to be significant.

All year she had been anticipating her Friday the 13th birthday. What if — knowing what she knew now — what if her real mother had been waiting for this birthday to make herself known?

Jo's heart leapt — then crashed. She shouldn't have jumped the gun. Maybe it was bad luck to cross out a day before it was over. To be on the safe side, she turned back to November and erased the X.

Breakfast was the Saturday morning special — a five-minute egg, a plate of hot buttered toast, a glass of fresh orange juice. She gave the egg a sharp whack with the edge of her spoon, peeled off the top, and began to eat.

"Have a good sleep?" Mom looked up from the newspaper and smiled.

"Same as usual."

"Know what, Jo?" Ian dipped a strip of toast into his egg and pointed it in her direction. "Know what? Wayne and me are going to the movies tonight. To see *Bambi*."

"Wayne and I. And stop waving that around. You're dripping egg yolk." Jo hadn't meant to snap. But did he have to be so annoying? If she heard one more "Know what?" she'd kill him.

Ian gulped down the toast. "His mom's taking us."

Jo scooped out the last of her egg. "Where's Dad?"

"He left early to get a start on that wiring job," Mom said. "Shocking, isn't it? To work on a Saturday."

"Shocking? Oh! I get it!" Ian laughed. "That's pretty funny, Mom."

Jo rolled her eyes and gave a loud sigh.

"What are you doing today, Jo?" Mom asked pleasantly.

Jo chewed on her toast and stared out the window. The ground was white with frost, and the sky was as clear and blue as Ian's purie marble. It was a day for doing something special.

"I've made a triple chocolate cake," Mom was saying. "I was all set to ice it, but wouldn't you know?

I'm out of icing sugar. So before you get settled on doing anything, will you go to the store for me?"

"No."

"I beg your pardon?"

"I have to be at Wendy's," Jo said impulsively. Wendy had given her a standing invitation to come over any Saturday morning to watch TV.

"You'll be sorry when there's no icing on the cake."

"No I won't. I hate chocolate cake anyway."

"That's a fine attitude."

"Tough."

Mom's mouth tightened. "I know you're angry. But that does not give you the right to be rude. Or to make everyone else miserable. You think you're a different person all of a sudden? You're not."

Jo started to get up, but Mom gripped her shoulder. "Wait! You hear me out. Yes, you're adopted. Yes, we should've told you. But this has gone far enough. You're not doing what I ask, you won't come to Grandma's with me, you're barely civil to anyone — I've had enough! Your father's had enough! If you think we're going to put up with this nonsense — if you think you can make us feel guilty for loving you — then you can think again. Is that clear? Talk to me! I'm still your mother!"

"No, you're not!" In one forceful move, Jo broke away. "And don't say you love me — you don't! You don't understand me, you don't even know me!" She hurled the words from across the room. "It's all lies, my whole life! And you're just a . . . a . . . *betrayer!*"

"Come back and talk to me!"

Jo grabbed her coat from the rack in the hall. "Don't be mad, Mom," Ian was saying, "I'll go to the store. Then I'll go to Wayne's. Can he come for lunch, Mom? For chocolate cake? Can he?"

"Jo —"

"You still don't get it, do you?" Jo shouted from the front door. "You're NOT my mother!"

"JO!"

The door slammed.

"Flicka! Get out of the way!" Jo tripped over the dog and almost fell down the stairs. She grabbed her bike, gave the tire a savage kick, and raced off to Wendy's.

Talk to her? She had *never* been able to talk to her. Whenever she wanted to know about something important, like sex, for instance, Mom turned red and mumbled about waiting till she was older. Talk to her? Ha!

Her *real* mother wouldn't be like that. Her real mother would be perfect. Perfect! She'd never get mad or make Jo do things she didn't want to do. Or yell at her because she wouldn't go to the store. She'd understand Jo, and know her better than she knew herself. She'd tell Jo everything, and be her best friend in the whole entire world.

Jo arrived at Wendy's with a stitch in her side from pedaling so hard. Only to discover that Wendy had gone downtown with her mom.

Well, good. She didn't really want to be cooped up inside, watching TV.

She rode back to her street and headed up the hill. The Featherstones' car wasn't in the driveway but

Michael might be home. And it was a great day for a bike ride. They could go to Beacon Hill Park, then along the waterfront — all the way to Willows Beach! It would be deserted this time of year, and if the tide was out they could bike on the hard sand, and beachcomb, and Michael could figure out the number of grains of sand —

Excited, she dropped her bike on his front lawn, hurried around to the back and knocked on the kitchen door. "Michael! It's me!"

She knocked again, louder. But it wasn't Michael who answered.

"Gil?" Jo gaped in surprise. "What are you —"

"Hey, guys!" Gil called over his shoulder. "It's the shark! Should we let her in?"

"Sure," Donny answered. "S'long as she doesn't bite."

Gil made a sweeping gesture with his arm. "Come on in, make yourself at home."

"Like it's your house. Where's Michael?"

"Upstairs getting his basketball," Bob said. "Too bad. You'll have to play by yourself today."

"Maybe not. Maybe I'll come with you guys. I can shoot baskets as good as you."

Gil gave her an admiring punch on the arm. "Yeah, you must be a great shot. All that target practice with Michael and his gun. Huh, Jo?"

"Michael!" she shouted. "Are you coming or what?"

"Is that it, Jo? You do target practice with Michael's gun?"

"Don't you morons ever stop? You are so pathetic."

"You hear about the game yesterday after school? The basketball game?" Bob mocked Jo's blank expression. "Duhh! The *tournament*, Gillespie. Oh, man, it was close. And Michael, our very own, very best player, scored the winning goal. You never heard, did you?"

"Yeah, I heard. Big hairy deal." Jo turned as the kitchen door opened and Michael appeared, spinning his basketball. "Michael, you want to —"

"Here he is!" Bob slapped Michael on the back. "The hero himself! Not only wins the game but the whole flippin' tournament. Hey, Mikey? How's it feel?"

Michael blushed and gave Jo a can't-help-if-I'm-famous kind of look. He faked a pass to Bob then did a behind-the-back pass to Donny.

"Hey, amigo!" Donny did a quick spin and returned the ball. "Jo was just saying what a good shot she is with your Wemley."

"Webley," Michael corrected. "You coming with us, Jo?"

Before she could answer, Gil said, "When can we see it? You're a hot-shot basketball star, let's see what a hot *shot* you are. Hey, buddy? Come on. We oughta celebrate."

Michael laughed. "You never give up, do you?" He dribbled the ball across the kitchen floor, weaving in and out amongst the boys. "Let's go."

"Ah, c'mon Mike," Donny pleaded. "We're not gonna touch it or anything."

"We're your friends," Bob said. "You're cool, let's have a look."

Jo glared. "Don't you guys understand English? He said, no!"

"C'mon Mike, be a sport!" The boys persisted. Cajoled and wheedled. Pat on the back. Nudge in the arm. Praise-the-hero squeeze around the shoulders.

Michael dodged. Side-stepped. Laughed it off. "No! You're wasting your breath!"

Jo stood by the kitchen sideboard and kept score. Three against one, but Michael was holding his own. Any minute now, the pit bulls would give up and go home.

Back and forth, advance, retreat.

At last they grew tired of the game. Gil said, "OK, if that's the way you want it. C'mon guys. Let's shoot baskets without him. He's got Jo to play with now."

Jo gave a silent cheer. Bike riding to Willows Beach! They could make sandwiches and have lunch on the beach. And use Alan's summer windbreak, if high tides hadn't swept it away. "Michael, do you —"

"Hey, Gil." Bob's loud voice bounced across the room. "I've got a coupla extra hockey tickets for tonight's game. You interested? Me and Donny are going. I was gonna ask Michael . . ."

"Who's playing?"

"Mich-*ael*." Jo plucked nervously at her coat sleeve. Why couldn't they just go?

"Victoria Cougars and Vancouver Canucks. Oh man, it's gonna be a great game. The Cougars are mad 'cause they got wiped in Vancouver last night, four-two. So tonight they're gonna even the score."

Michael grinned. "I'd love to see the Cougars get even."

"One last chance, Featherstone. You want a hockey ticket? Show us the gun."

For a long moment, all eyes were on Michael. He held the basketball in his hands as if weighing a decision, then said, "All right. I'll show you the gun."

20

"Don't be an idiot!" Jo blurted out. "You can't get the gun! You —"

Something in Michael's eyes made her stop. It was a look that said, Don't push me any further. At the same time, it begged her to understand. "Relax, Jo," Michael said. "It won't hurt just to look."

"Yeah, Jo. Stop being a spoilsport."

"Just go home, why doncha?"

Jo stared at the kitchen linoleum. It was ugly — squares and rectangles in shades of blue and brown. She traced the smallest square with the toe of her shoe. Should she go? Should she stay? She heard Michael climb the stairs and open the study door. She knew he would get the gun. She knew why.

Her toe traced a bigger square. It wouldn't end with Michael *showing* the gun. The boys would want to hold it. Then load it. Then . . .

Why didn't she go home? She'd feel safe there.

The thought came so unexpectedly her toe stopped in mid-square. For the first time in weeks, home was where she wanted to be.

But she couldn't go home. Not now. Not when she'd left in such a rage. If Dad was home, maybe. But her mother . . .

"Wow! This is the real thing!" Gil was the first to react when Michael returned. "Hey, good buddy! Just lemme touch it, OK? Thank you, ol' pal of mine." He ran his finger along the barrel, then grasped the butt with both hands. "Geez! It's heavy!"

"Everyone can have a turn holding it," Michael said. "Then I'll put it away."

"Coo-ol!" Bob held the grip and pointed at Donny. "Bang! You're dead."

"Aughh!" Donny gave an exaggerated performance of dying on the linoleum, right at Jo's feet. "Help me, please . . . Aughh!" He clutched his heart and waved his legs in the air. "Show mercy, Jo. Mercy! Aughh, the pain. Don't be cruel . . ."

Michael laughed with the other boys. "See, Mike," Gil said. "There's no problem. You should've shown us months ago."

Jo moved away, disgusted. "Better put it back before your parents get home." No one was listening. She spoke more loudly. "Michael, your parents! It's almost noon! They'll be home for lunch."

"It's quarter past ten." Bob waved the gun in her face. "Can't you tell time yet?"

"What's the lever for?" Donny rose from the dead and took the gun from Bob. He pressed the lever on the side and pulled down on the barrel. "This is how you load it, huh, Mike?"

"Well, actually —"

"Hey! What's this?" Gil had stepped over to the sideboard and was standing by an open drawer. He held up a small box.

"Give me that!" Michael lunged towards him but Gil dodged out of the way and tossed the box to Bob.

"Bull's eye!" Bob caught the box and opened it. "Cartridges! Pointy end first, right?" Before anyone could stop him, he snatched the gun from Donny and placed a cartridge in the cylinder. Then he pushed up on the barrel and locked it in place.

"Bloody hell!" Michael said angrily. "You better give it back! My parents —"

"Ah, Mikey!" Gil cuffed his shoulder. "Don't get upset. Just one shot, OK? Just to try it."

"You want the hockey ticket?" said Bob.

"Yeah, Mike. How about it? Just one shot. OK, amigo?"

Michael made a grab for the gun, but before he could reach it, Bob had spun around and handed it to Gil.

"This sucker's loaded!" Gil cradled it in both hands and ran upstairs to the study, the others fast on his heels.

Jo ran, too. The scene was horribly familiar, as if

she'd played it in her mind, talked it out as a story, written it down. And because she didn't know what happened next, she had no choice but to be swept along.

"Don't touch the trigger!" Michael was yelling. "Whatever you do, keep your finger off it!"

"See that oak tree across the street?" Gil flung open the window. "How about I aim for that? Hey, Mike? Think I can hit the tree?"

"There's a lady in the yard," Bob said. "Better wait til she's outta the way."

"She's going in already." Gil placed his finger on the trigger and began to pull it back.

"Don't," Michael pleaded. "I told you — Look, you pull back too far, you can't stop! There's no going back!"

Jo's heart pounded. Blood hammered in her head. It felt as if the world had stopped turning. But that couldn't be. How could it, when everything was spinning so fast?

She should have done something. Grabbed the gun as soon as Michael brought it downstairs. Taken it home. But she'd missed her chance. Gil would shoot it. Someone else would want a turn. They'd all want a turn.

"Whaddya want me to hit?" Gil asked. "The trunk or that branch up top?"

"Maybe you better put it down." Donny reached for the gun.

"Take a powder!" Gil said. "I'm not gonna hurt anything. Whaddya think I am, crazy?"

"Please, Gil," said Michael. "Give me the gun. You can't —"

Then everyone was shouting at once.

"Hold it! There's a kid on a bike!"

"I know that kid —"

"There's another one coming."

"Jo! Get back!"

Jo lunged for the gun.

Suddenly, the gun went off. A deafening explosion roared through the room.

Jo gagged on the stench of gunpowder and swallowed the sickening taste in her throat. Her legs trembled.

She heard voices outside. The high-pitched, Saturday-morning voices of boys on bikes, coasting down the hill. Through the cloud of blue-black smoke she caught a glimpse of a wheel, a blur of colored foil. Milk bottle caps, folded over the spokes.

Around her, the others began to stir. Slowly. Shakily.

"Oh, god."

"Must've gone —"

"Wild. I guess. Hit the tree high up, maybe?"

"Oh, god."

"Least it didn't —" Gil's face was white. "Those kids — Oh, god. Hey, Jo? It's all right."

Something snapped. "*All right?*" she screamed. "That was my brother! He could've been shot — any one of us could've been shot! And killed!"

"Jo, calm down. It's over."

She whirled around to Michael. "You're right, it's over. Give me that." She snatched the box of cartridges from his hand and rammed it into her coat pocket. Then fled down the stairs.

She was picking up her bike when Michael's parents pulled into the driveway. She started to tell, wanted to tell, but the words jammed up in her throat. It wasn't up to her, anyway. Let Michael tell. It was his fault.

She leapt on her bike and flew down the hill without touching the brakes. Past her house, past the bikes thrown down on the lawn — which meant Ian and Wayne were inside. Had they heard the shot? Seen the bullet? Felt it whiz by? Were they now, right this minute, telling Mom?

She sailed through the stop sign, across the street, into the woods. Only then did she start pedaling. Up the slope, crusty with frost. Past the frozen pond, through the tunnel of grim, leafless branches, out onto the busy street.

Instead of going ahead to the school, she turned right and pedaled hard along Bay Street. She rode without seeing the familiar houses and yards and buildings, the Bay Street Armoury with its turrets and tanks. As she pedaled she heard the jangling sound of cartridges in her pocket.

She reached the Point Ellice Bridge, rode halfway across, then stopped against the railing, breathing hard. Her side hurt, her eyes were watering, she needed to blow her nose — but it wasn't for that she stopped.

With cold, fumbling fingers she took the box of cartridges from her pocket and hurled it far out over the water.

The box opened as it fell. Cartridges spilled out and glinted in the sun. Cold metal. Silver-gold. One by one they hit the water and sank beneath the surface.

She watched until no trace remained. Only the empty box, floating on the tide.

Jo kept on going. Without thinking, she crossed the bridge, veered right onto Craigflower Road and into Victoria West. As soon as she spotted the church steeple, she knew where she was heading. At the church she turned onto a quiet avenue. A brown shingle house stood halfway down the street, with a cedar hedge and two giant rhododendrons.

Inside, the house was warm and smelled of ginger-snaps. Jo found her grandfather in his worn leather chair, listening to the news on the radio. "Yoanne!" he exclaimed in his Swedish accent. "*Min lilla hönsa hoppa.* What a surprise, my little jumping hen." He called to the kitchen, "Lydia! Look who's here!"

Grandma came out wiping floury hands on her apron. "My, oh my! Just look at my girl!" She wrapped Jo in a hug. "You came by yourself? On your bike? It's a month since we've seen you. A month! Come into the kitchen, now. We'll have a cup of tea." She helped Jo with her coat and sat her down at the kitchen table.

Grandad poured the tea and offered Jo a ginger-snap. "Fresh out of the oven. Your grandma must have known you were coming."

"She's not my grandma." The words came out in a rush. "And Mom's not my real mom. And I can't go home because we had a fight and . . . and then at Michael's they were fooling around with the gun and it went off and Ian, I was so scared, Ian was almost shot. I knew it — I never should've changed the calendar before it was time. I knew it. He could've been killed. Or Michael, or any of us. I was so scared."

She ached. A hard, heavy ache as if the gun were lodged deep in her throat, her chest, her belly, the gun and the bullets, about to explode. If she could cry, the ache might go away. But she couldn't.

Grandma drew her close and rocked her back and forth. "There, there, let's take things one bit at a time. Your mama knows you're here? No? And the gun — at Michael's, was it? Yes? All right. John, phone Cathy and tell her everything."

"I don't want to go home." Jo's breath caught in a sob. "Can I spend the night here?"

"Yes, yes. If it's all right with your mama." Grandma spoke softly, smoothing Jo's hair. "Hard enough just growing up without all this. Your mama, when she was your age? Oh, the tears. The crying. Up one minute, down the next. Most of the time for no reason."

Jo's bottom lip quivered. "She never told me. All this time. I thought she was my mom."

"Yes, she told us you'd found out. About time, too."

"Who's ready for another cup?" Grandad returned to the kitchen and poured more tea, then passed Jo the gingersnaps. "Have one. Go on. You'll feel better."

"No, John. Save the gingersnaps for after. It's lunch time. Soup is what she needs, some good beef vegetable soup. It'll be ready now." Grandma got up and ladled soup from the pot simmering on the oil stove.

Jo's stomach churned. "Grandad, when you phoned, did you say anything about Ian? And the gun?"

He patted her hand. "Don't you worry. Ian and his friend — Wayne, is it? — they said they heard a bang but thought it was a neighbor's car backfiring. They had no idea. Michael told his parents. Your mama went up and talked to them. And she talked to the boys — they're very upset. The police came, too. Michael's father gave them the gun. All that's left is the cartridges."

"No," Jo said. "I threw them off the bridge." She swallowed a spoonful of soup. Grandma was right. It was good.

"Your mama's worried about you," Grandad said. "Are you sure you want to stay the night?"

Jo nodded. It was too soon to face her mother after what she'd said at breakfast.

"Mmm —" Grandma slurped noisily. "*Utmärkt!* I don't remember much Swedish after all these years, but delicious food is *utmärkt!* Yes, *min lilla hönsa hoppa.* All this about Mom not being your real mom. Who changed your diapers and bandaged your cut fingers? Hmm? Who sat up with you when you were sick or having nightmares? I know, I know. Suddenly everything's topsy-turvy."

Topsy-turvy. Turns on a dime. Swept away by an avalanche. Jo pushed the words out of her head.

"More soup? No? Have another cup of tea, then. And a gingersnap. Go on, take as many as you like." Grandma leaned forward in her chair, her arms resting on the table. "Remember I told you how I loved to dance in the midnight sun? When I was a girl in Sweden? And you and Ian made the picture for my birthday? I'm going to tell you the rest of the story."

Jo took another bite of the crisp gingersnap. It had nothing to do with her, this story. Nothing to do with who she was or where she came from. But Grandma's voice was as warm and inviting as her old patchwork quilt. Jo snuggled into it, content to listen.

21

"When I was born, my mother wasn't married." Grandma chuckled at Jo's shocked expression. "It's true! We lived with my grandparents on their farm. My mother hated the sight of me. Why? Because I was always there to remind her of her mistake. But my grandmother? Oh, she was the world to me.

"Then one day, out of the blue, my father shows up. He'd turned religious. Decided he would marry my mother after all. I was six years old when they took me away. Oh, how I cried.

"My mother had more children. I was the oldest, so I had to look after the whole lot of them. I was treated like a servant.

"My father was very strict. Playing cards was

forbidden because he believed the devil was under the table. Music was forbidden, except for hymns. Books were forbidden, except for the Bible. Dancing was forbidden. But I loved to dance.

"One Midsummer Eve, when everyone in the house was asleep, I climbed out my bedroom window. I was thirteen, fourteen maybe, a little older than you. I ran like mischief to the village. Everyone was celebrating. I danced and danced in the midnight sun. Then I hurried home and climbed back through the window."

There was a long pause while Grandma took the bubbling kettle off the stove and refilled the teapot.

Jo helped herself to another gingersnap. "Did they find out?" she asked.

"Oh, yes. My father was waiting in my room. He took his belt with the buckle and beat me so hard I couldn't move for a week. But that didn't stop me. All summer long I stole away and danced in the midnight sun. I started to think, I can go my own way in the world. So when I had the chance to come to Canada, I was ready.

"A friend sent me a ticket. I was twenty. Couldn't speak a word of English. And what I knew about the world would fit in a thimble."

"You must have been afraid."

"Yes, but you know, there's worse things than being afraid. Like never being afraid. Because that means you never take risks. I took a risk and came to Canada. And met your grandfather." She smiled at him across the table. "Quite the risk, eh, John?"

Grandad chuckled. "Tell her about her Aunt Karin."

Jo frowned. "I don't know — oh." She had a hazy recollection of old photographs in her grandmother's album. One showed a woman — Karin — in a long dress sitting at an easel with paintbrush in hand. The other showed Grandma and Karin standing together in front of a train station. "Aunt Karin — she was old, wasn't she?"

"Not always!" Grandma laughed. "John, get that box of photos, the ones from the mountains."

Jo wondered what any of this had to do with her. Family stories wrapped up in a box. Once she would have pored over the faded photos, searching for connections, for threads that linked those lives with hers. Past lives? More like past lies.

At last Grandma found what she was looking for. She handed Jo a photo showing a large crowd of people posed around a locomotive. There were several children, men in three-piece suits with watch chains looped across their vests, and women in long dresses and fancy hats.

"Oh, for gosh sakes." Grandad smiled and pointed to a girl in front. "There's little Karin."

The girl looked to be Jo's age. She wore a long-sleeved white dress with a lace collar. A wide-brimmed straw hat trimmed with flowers sat rakishly on her head. One arm was a blur, as if she'd raised it to wave at someone just as the picture was taken. The photographer, maybe? Jo couldn't quite make out the expression on her face. Was it mischief? Or impatience, to get to wherever they were going?

"Karin was my daughter," Grandad said. "The woman next to her was my first wife, Karin's mother. She died in an avalanche when Karin was twelve."

"The avalanche you were in?"

"No, that came later."

Jo concentrated on the woman in the photo. One hand held a large bouquet of flowers. The other was tucked through the arm of the man standing beside her. "So this . . ." Jo touched the tall, fair-haired figure and looked up at her grandfather. "This must be you."

"Yes, that's your grandad," Grandma said. "Wasn't he handsome? And Karin . . . I was just eight years older. When I first arrived she taught me English and showed me around the town. She took me hiking in the mountains. We became friends, like sisters. And two years later I married her papa.

"Can you imagine, being a mother to someone so close to my own age? I was afraid, you know. I never let it show, not to John, not to anyone. I was afraid Karin would hate me for trying to take her mother's place. But she didn't. No, not a bit of it."

Jo reached for another gingersnap and chewed thoughtfully, staring at the photograph. When Karin posed for the camera that day, had she any idea how her life was about to change? Had her mother? Or father?

The thought reminded her of Rogers Pass. "Grandad, you know the avalanche, when you went to make the phone call? I always thought an angel whispered in your ear, to make sure you went at the right time. I thought — I thought you were saved for a reason. And that reason had to do with Mom being born. So I could be born. But it didn't matter, did it? Because I would have been born anyway."

Grandad smiled. "That may be. But if it wasn't for the mother who adopted you, you wouldn't be sitting here eating the best gingersnaps in the world."

That afternoon, Jo challenged Grandad to a few games of crib, played the piano for a while, then worked on the hooked rug she'd started in the summer. Long red strips cut from an old flannel shirt, purple from a tweed jacket, orange and blue from heaven-knew-where. She punched the hook into the burlap backing, caught a loop from a strip of cloth held underneath, and pulled it through. It was satisfying to watch the flowers bloom beneath her fingers.

She found a strip of yellow from a baby blanket and started hooking a midnight sun. She would frame it with navy blue.

After dinner, Grandad lit a fire in the fireplace and put on one of his special logs. A Yule log that burned colored flames.

Jo curled up on the chesterfield and watched the flames waver and dance. Green, turquoise, purple and red. The log smelled of pine. And Christmas.

Three pictures hung above the mantle. Two paintings of mountains, and in the center, *Dancing in the Midnight Sun*.

"The frame you made looks good, Grandad," Jo said.

"Not as good as your picture. Karin did those oil paintings, the ones of the mountains. Did I ever tell you that?"

"No." There was so much Jo didn't know. "She died, didn't she? Aunt Karin."

"Yes, when you were a baby. She was only fifty-nine. It's too bad. You would have liked her."

"I used to like Mack," Jo said. "I was going to give her the rug I'm making for a Christmas present. I'm not, now." She felt a flare of anger, hot and snapping. "I hate her! The whole time, she was using me as an excuse to go out and meet her stupid boyfriends. Then she got into trouble. Then she had to tell me I was adopted."

"All the same, you'll be sorry to see her go."

"Nope. I won't even say good-bye."

"When I left Sweden," Grandma said, "I never said good-bye to my father. I never regretted it, either. You know the expression, blood is thicker than water? Don't believe it. I was glad to see the last of my father. But with you and Mack it's different."

"But she —"

"Yes, yes, she hurt you. But don't forget all the times she made you happy. You be sure to say good-bye, one way or another."

22

Jo was glad of the wind. Glad to feel it whip her face, sting her cheeks, whirl inside her head. If it blew hard enough, it could untangle her thoughts and blow them away. Blow them away to the mountains. Blow them over the water and out to sea.

Dad had phoned earlier that morning and offered to pick her up, but Jo declined. She wanted the cold, the long bike ride home. She wanted the wind.

And clouds. Heavy, billowing, avalanche clouds, darkening from white to gray to purple, raced her across the bridge and along the street, teasing her with a promise of snow.

If it got cold enough, it could freeze her thoughts. Turn them into one solid block of ice. Then she could chip away, bit by bit by bit until the last thought was gone.

Her fingertips were freezing, in spite of the mittens Grandma insisted she wear. But it wasn't cold enough. Or windy enough. Thoughts still popped and hissed in her skull like the crackle of Grandad's Yule log fire. Except that her thoughts didn't blaze in stop-the-heart colors. They were gray and cold, like the ashes left in the grate.

Her family story was one blank page. Jo could write it, but how? How could she find the beginning?

Fine for Grandma to say, "Blood's not thicker than water." Grandma knew her blood.

Fine for Aunt Karin to have a generous heart and welcome Grandma into the family. Aunt Karin lost her mother. But at least she had known her.

Fine for Grandma to say Mom did this and Mom did that. Was Jo supposed to feel grateful? Mom — and Dad — did all that parent stuff because they wanted to. It was their choice. Fine. Except that Jo never got to pick.

Another four blocks and she'd be home. Dad had said Mom wanted to talk to her. It didn't take a brilliant mind to figure out what that little talk would be about.

The music took Jo by surprise.

She heard it as she approached the house, recognized the Schumann melody, and leaned against the weeping willow to listen.

Although she hadn't played it for a long time, the piece was one of her favorites. Her mother's, too —

one Mom had played when she was a young girl. She was playing it now.

Dolce e cantabile. A haunting melody, lilting and mysterious. *Andante.*

The music ended, then started again.

Jo's fingers began to move. Inside the woolen mittens, her fingers unerringly touched the keys, reached for the sharps and flats, captured the smooth *legato* phrasing in harmony with her mother.

How long had it been since she and Mom had sat side by side on the piano bench and played together? Giggled over the wrong notes, raced up and down octaves, traded parts in duets without missing a beat? How long since they'd shared the joy of making music? In spite of everything, they did have that in common. They did have that connection.

In spite of everything.

Slow now, slow, *ritardando.*

Jo heard the music build to the lovely *crescendo*, felt her mother's fingers pause, waiting, as hers did — then the soft *pianissimo*, quietly, quietly fading away. Leaving a shimmering silence. An ache. A longing.

When Jo went inside, her mother was still sitting at the piano. Not playing, but staring off into space. Tears streamed down her cheeks.

"Mom?" Jo hesitated at the door. Her stomach squirmed. Did her mother want to be caught crying? Probably not. Probably Jo should ignore her and go to her room. "I'm just . . ."

"Wait." Mom turned to her. "All I wanted, all I ever wanted was to be a good mother. I tried. I tried the best

I knew how."

Her voice was small, her breathing ragged. "I was afraid I'd lose you. If I told you about the adoption. I was afraid — and when I heard about the gun and thought what could've happened . . ."

Jo couldn't speak.

Mom raised a hand, as if she wanted to reach out to Jo and draw her in. But she let it fall, and turned back to the piano.

Suddenly the ache was unbearable. All the anger, betrayal, hurt — all of it — erupted in one tremendous sob that tore a hole in Jo's heart. She rushed to her mother, clung to her, and cried.

Some moments are caught in slow motion.

Jo lay her head in the hollow of her mother's shoulder and felt the weight of those moments. *Largo. Adagio.* Every detail pressed out and preserved like the wildflowers she'd kept between the pages of a book.

Dust motes in sunlight. Mom's brown hair, trailing an S curve over the blue collar of her dress. The dry rustle of a begonia leaf falling to the hardwood floor. Fish chowder simmering in the kitchen, the pungent smell of the sea.

In that slow motion of time, Jo felt suspended. Held between the person she was and the person she might have been. Held between the mother she knew and the mother she might never know.

"I don't want to lose you," Mom said quietly. "So

I'll let you go, if your heart's so set on knowing. When you're ready. When the time comes."

The words were a revelation. She does know me, Jo thought. In spite of everything.

"You have to realize, it may not be possible. The adoption laws — there's no easy access. And it's a huge risk. She — the woman who had you — might not want to be found. It may take years. Maybe forever."

Jo didn't care. Her mother had opened the door. It was a gift.

23

Jo's birthday was full of surprises.

Sharon, in an attack of on-again friendship, brought a cake to school. It was roughly in the shape of a grand piano, with a keyboard in lemon and chocolate icing. Jo's name was written in metallic blue. The class sang "Happy Birthday" and Mr. West gave them a no-homework day. Everyone cheered, until Gil reminded them that Mr. West never gave homework on Fridays anyway.

Grandma and Grandad took Jo and her family to dinner at the Net Loft, Victoria's newest restaurant. Michael came, too. The restaurant was on the harbor, close to the Parliament Buildings and CPR wharf. The best thing about it, even better than the view of passing ships, was the *smörgasbord*. In true Swedish tradition, a long table was set with a variety of dishes — herring served with potatoes, sour cream and onions; marinated salmon, shrimp, prawns, and crab; salads; roast beef and turkey. And those were just the cold dishes. After the various hot dishes, including Swedish meatballs, came the dessert table.

Ian couldn't believe they were supposed to serve themselves. Whatever they wanted, however much they wanted — that's how it worked. Jo suggested that Mom skip the *Chatelaine* Meals of the Month and do *smörgasbords* instead.

When they got home, Jo opened her gifts. Everyone gave her something, even Flicka.

"Oh, what a good girl!" Jo exclaimed after unwrapping the shiny red leash. "You're going to take me for walks now, is that it? Eh, girl?" She gave the dog a hug and got a wet kiss in return.

The last gift was a surprise from Grandma and Grandad.

"You already gave me something," Jo said, pointing to the traditional box of chocolates.

"Yes, but this isn't from us." Grandad handed Jo a small blue box. "This is from your Aunt Karin. She left it for you."

"She wanted you to have it on your sixteenth birthday," Grandma said. "But your grandad and I think now is a good time. Go ahead. Open it."

Jo opened the box. Inside was a pendant — a coppery-red stone attached to a thin golden chain.

"Wow!" Ian peered over Jo's shoulder. "It's better than any of my marbles. Do you think —"

"No! Not in a million years." Jo held it up to the light. The stone was the color of the sun, the way she'd seen it sometimes, just before it disappeared behind the hills. When she twirled it, gold flakes flickered and shone. "It's beautiful."

"It's called a goldstone," Grandad said. "It belonged to Karin's mother. She was wearing it when the avalanche came, when she was swept away. It was lost for a time, until Karin found it in the snow."

Jo ran her finger over the smooth, polished stone. "Why did — why me?"

"Karin had a way of knowing things," Grandad said. "She must have felt you might need the goldstone one day.

"Can I . . ." She held up the pendant.

"Yes, put it on, but be careful of the chain. It was broken twice in the same spot. A weak link, I suppose. But it's together now."

Jo smiled. The goldstone was like a message from her aunt, saying, You are a part of our family.

She promised herself she would always wear the pendant. It would be like having a link to Karin. Like having a guardian angel.

Later, Mack brought over a Baked Alaska with twelve candles. Jo made a wish before she blew them out.

She didn't wish that her real mother would appear out of the blue.

She didn't wish that she would one day find her.

Not that Jo *didn't* want those wishes to come true. But since Mom had said she *could* search — and possibly find — that was enough for now. Besides, there were connections in this home, in this family, worth keeping. She knew her real mother was just that — *real*. A person. Not a fairy godmother who would whisk Jo away to Fantasyland.

So her wish, when it came, surprised her.

Like most good wishes, it was for something possible, but not guaranteed. Something just a bit out of reach. A wish that — if granted — would bring a touch of magic.

It might have been the goldstone that put the idea in Jo's head. Or the thought of connections. And Aunt Karin.

Whatever the reason, she wished for snow.

24

It was the quiet that woke Jo in the middle of the night. A quiet that muffled the familiar hum of the neighborhood. A quiet that could mean only one thing.

Eagerly, she sat up and pulled back the curtains. At last, after two long months, her wish had come true.

By seven o'clock, Ian was up and yelling, "Snow! It's snowing! And it's Saturday!" He bolted down his pancakes and waited impatiently for Jo to finish hers. "Hurry up! We've got to get on the toboggan before it all melts! Hey, Dad? Can we?"

"It's below freezing out there," Dad reminded him. "It's not going to melt for a while. And as soon as everyone's finished breakfast, we'll all go for a run. Toboggan run, that is." He winked at Mom and poured her a second cup of coffee.

Jo mopped up the maple syrup on her plate and gulped down her orange juice. "Look out the window, Dad. See, Mom? No car tracks. There's not even any footprints. We'll be the first on the hill. Ian, are you coming? We'll go and warm up the toboggan."

She was halfway out the door when the phone rang. "It's snowing!" Michael's voice cracked with excitement. "Six inches and still coming down. It's like we're *really* in Canada! But it's unusual, isn't it, for this time of year? Jo? Are you there? I thought by the middle of February —"

"Stop talking! I'll meet you outside."

"I haven't had breakfast yet. Are you going —"

"Michael! Good-bye!"

Jo was right. They were first on the hill. "Keep your voices down," Dad whispered. "No one will know."

They pulled the toboggan up the hill, leaving one smooth white path, four pairs of footprints, one set of pawprints. By the time they reached the top, the falling snow had already covered their tracks.

"We're like ghost walkers," Mom said softly.

Jo liked that. She could use it in a story.

"Can we wake everybody up now?" Ian hopped from one foot to the other.

Dad chuckled. "Don't know about you, but I don't know how anybody can keep quiet on a toboggan."

They got on, Ian in front, then Jo, Mom and Dad. Flicka cavorted from one to the other, licking each face and barking with excitement.

"Everybody ready?" Dad said. "Hold on tight!"

"Wait, wait!" Jo said. "We need a rallying cry. Something like —"

"Bombs away!" Ian shouted.

"No, wait — I've got it. Avalanche! OK? When we push off, everybody yell avalanche."

"Here we go then. Ready, set . . ."

"AVALAAANCHE!"

The toboggan whooshed down the hill.

Jo caught her breath. For one long sweeping moment there was nothing but the rush, the exhilaration, the joy of flying through a whirlwind of snow. Swirling flakes tickled her eyes, her nose, her cheeks, and melted on the tip of her tongue.

"Hang on!" Ian plowed the toboggan into a soft drift of snow. They tumbled out, giddy with laughter.

Flicka pranced around, snuffling, yapping, wagging her tail, planting slobbery kisses.

"Let's go again!" Ian exclaimed. "It's like being in a snow globe, isn't it, Jo? You know, like that one we shake at Christmas?"

"You're right." Jo smiled. They were all in a snow globe, part of a miniature scene stirred up and shaken to a blizzard. And when the shaking had stopped, when they tumbled into the drift, before they started getting up, there was a moment of stillness as the falling snow settled over them. In spite of all the shaking, the scene hadn't changed. They were still together. And maybe that was it. Her wish. The magic of snow.

By the time they reached the top, the hill was awake and in a holiday mood. Neighbors of all ages were shoveling walks, building snowmen, digging sleds out of basements. Snow was the only topic of conversation. How long would it last? Would this snowfall beat the record? When would the city send out the sanding trucks?

Michael joined them for the next run. After that, Mom and Dad went inside and left the toboggan for the kids.

"Avalanche!" Jo clasped Michael's waist as the toboggan flew down the hill, over and over again. Friends from school came and went and came back for more. They raced them on sleds, pelted them with snowballs as they streaked past, and were pelted in turn.

Jo allowed herself to be lured inside for lunch, but was out again within minutes. A snowball fight, face-washing attacks, advice to Ian and Wayne on building a snowfort, then back to the toboggan.

By mid-afternoon, the sky had cleared. Ice crystals danced in the sunlight. The hill, trees, houses — everything gleamed. There was a newness to the world, a whiteness, a brightness, a sparkle, like a gift wrapped in shiny paper. A gift to be tucked away, Jo thought. To be opened whenever she wanted to remember the surprise of the snow.

At night, the temperature fell. Snow gathered in the cold and held it. Before long, Jo and Michael were the only ones left on the hill.

"We haven't made snow angels yet," Jo said. "Come on." She led Michael to the woods behind the fort, where the snow lay deep and undisturbed.

They flung themselves on their backs, moving arms and legs in wide sweeping arcs. "There's just one problem," Michael said. "How do we get up without demolishing them?"

"We don't." Jo laughed. "We stay here forever." She lay back in the snow, breathing in the silver glitter of sky, the mystery of stars.

Mystery. That was the School Board's topic for the next Composition Award. Jo figured most kids would write detective stories, with clues and suspects and titles like "The Mystery of the Emerald Shark." She would write about something different. Life, for instance. That was a mystery. You never knew what was going to happen. And when it did, you hardly ever knew why.

She thought about Mack, way off in Toronto. Jo was glad she'd taken Grandma's advice and said good-bye. She'd made a true confession — told Mack how she had always wanted to grow up and be like her. How she had even changed her name, thinking if beautiful and perfect Susan MacKenzie Lamont could be just plain Mack, then Joanne Catherine Gillespie could be Jo. Now, she just wanted to be herself. Mack had hugged her and said, "Good for you. That's the best person you can possibly be."

Jo thought of Mack's baby. Three months to go, and someone would be taking that baby home. Another mystery.

Maybe Jo would write her own family story. All the unanswered questions, dreamlike figures, nameless voices . . . Mom had said, "Whenever you're ready.

When you feel the time is right."

Yes, Jo would begin the search and one day solve that mystery. But not now.

"How many stars?" Michael's voice broke into her thoughts.

"More than a million."

"Maybe a trillion?"

"Maybe."

"Actually, there's at least one sextillion. That's a one followed by thirty-six zeros."

"Oh, Michael. Honestly."

He reached across the spread of wings and held her hand. Through the layers of wooly mittens she could feel his warmth. It shone through her, making her heart leap and her cheeks glow.

Unaccountably, her eyes welled up with tears. The stars blurred out of focus. She blinked, and the sky was bright with angels.

More novels by Julie Lawson

White Jade Tiger / Beach Holme Publishers
Cougar Cove / Orca Book Publishers
Goldstone / Stoddart Kids
Fires Burning / Stoddart